FYREBYRNE ISLAND:

BOOK ONE OF THE RACHAYA SERIES

Second edition published 2021. First published 2017.

NATIONAL LIBRARY OF AUSTRALIA

A catalogue record for this book is available from the National Library of Australia

Published by Ash Oldfield
ash@asholdfield.com

Editing by Kat Betts, Element Editing Services
Layout and book design by Assemblo Pty Ltd.
Second edition cover design by Franzi Haase
www.coverdungeon.com - Instagram: @coverdungeonrabbit
Map designed by Soraya Corcoran

ISBN 978-0-9874450-3-2

To Steve, for always sharing in the magic.

The Known Lands of Escoria

A M B R I'I A N   R A N G E

Great Gri'ikon

Cri'ikon

anjot

Tolsten

Paxley

Little d'hor

Andri'im Forest

K   D'H O R

Khaxtor

able Mist

CHAPTER 1

JOURNEY TO THE
IMPENETRABLE MIST

Bale Shearer swaggered triumphantly through the gates of Cryll. He made straight for the village inn and threw his rucksack into the middle of a table occupied by three drunken men.

'There you go, lads, I did it.' Pride gleamed from his craggy face. 'I made it all the way to the Impenetrable Mist and back.' He took a seat among them, grabbed a tankard and began filling it with ale.

The two older men merely rolled their eyes, but young Jed Tanner's eyes widened with excitement.

'Did you really, Bale? Did you pass *through* the Mist?'

'Don't be stupid, boy, how could I? It's impenetrable. That means you can't get through it.' He slapped the lad on the back of the head for good measure.

Saul Baker, the most senior of the men at the table, had been scratching his grey beard thoughtfully while Bale had been talking. Now he fixed Shearer with a disbelieving glare. 'Then what was the point of you going, eh? What dangers did you face? Alls I can see is that you took a leisurely Firesday stroll.'

Shearer spluttered into his warm ale. 'I'll have you know I faced many dangers – many *great* dangers. I was lucky to return with my skin intact and my eyes unharmed.'

'Oh yeah? And what were these dangers?' asked Saul. 'An overly frisky gouloub cub, perhaps?'

The table erupted into laughter.

Bale Shearer's wrinkled face turned beet red and he scowled at the men. 'Witches,' he said with relish.

Reg Chandler, a large, beefy man whose strong muscle had long since turned to fat, guffawed and slapped his meaty thigh. 'Now I know you're having us on, Shearer. Witches aren't real.'

Bale slammed his fist down on the table, making the ale slosh up and down in their tankards. 'They are real, I tell you, and I'll take a pound of flesh from any man who says it isn't so.'

Chandler shot to his feet to meet the challenge. 'Where do witches come from, eh?'

'The Lands Beyond the Impenetrable Mist, you stooge,' Shearer said.

'If the Mists are so impenetrable, how do witches get through them?' Saul Baker asked quietly, not quite as drunk as the other men.

'They use magic, of course, given to them by demons straight out of the Otherworld in exchange for their souls.' Bale Shearer raised his hands to his head and used his fingers to create horns on either side of his forehead. He stuck his tongue out for extra emphasis.

Jed Tanner's face went pale. 'I wouldn't want to meet with one of them,' he said.

'Well then it's lucky it's me that had to face them and not a coward like you, eh lad?' Shearer said.

Far from feeling insulted, Jed nodded in agreement and relief.

'Remember the butcher's wife? She that died when the Boldon fever hit the village?' Reg Chandler asked.

'Adara? I liked her,' said Jed. 'It was she that set me leg when I fell from the barn roof. Gave me a lovely drink of herbs to take away the pain and all, she did.'

'That's right,' said Chandler. 'No-one knows where she came from, do they? Just appeared one day. And how'd she know to set young

Tanner's leg like that? Aint no physik that's taught her that. A physik would've cut it clean off.'

'What are you implyin'?' Baker asked, turning gravely serious. 'The butcher's wife was a good woman.'

'A good woman, aye. Very carin' of others,' said Bale Shearer. His eyes widened in his wrinkled face with horror. 'What if she made the ultimate sacrifice? Sellin' her soul to wicked demons, just so she could save young Tanner's leg?'

The men fell silent, the gentle clink of tankards on wood the only noises to be heard.

Saul Baker was the first to break their reverie. 'No, we would have known if Adara had sold her soul to demons. She was unchanged after she treated Tanner. She was still as lovely as can be, right up until the day she died.'

The men nodded their agreement.

'What if she didn't sell her soul? What if she gave up something else as payment instead?'

'What do you mean, Shearer?' Saul asked.

'I mean – well, you've all heard the old stories,' Bale said, looking at each of the men to help him explain. The three men looked back at him blankly.

'Oh, come on, men! You know the stories as well as I. Of people selling their first-born children to evil spirits in exchange for magical favours.'

Baker shook his head emphatically. 'You mean young Rachaya and I cannot allow it. She's a nice girl from a well-respected family.'

'It stands to reason, though,' said young Jed with tears in his eyes. 'She's the spitting image of her mother, with her odd red hair and skinniness.' He dabbed at his eyes with a grimy handkerchief. 'That poor little girl. The demons must be waitin' till she's the right age, then they'll snatch her away in the night.'

'Or possess her,' said Shearer. 'Poor Butcher!'

Saul Baker's face had gone very white. 'Young Rachaya's turning thirteen next week – her father's ordered a cake from the bakery to celebrate.'

Reg Chandler leapt to his feet again, this time knocking over an entire pitcher of ale with his protruding stomach. 'We have to help her! We have to help that little girl! We cannot allow the demons to take the butcher's daughter.'

Baker nodded solemnly, wiping ale from his trousers. 'Yes, we must put a stop to this if we can.' He looked across expectantly at Shearer.

'Bale, you say you met with witches on your journey. Did they give any clues as to what might be done to prevent demons?'

Bale Shearer started to tremble, his hand shaking so hard that ale spilt over the rim of his tankard. 'Nay, Baker, don't ask that question of me,' he said.

'Shearer, if you have a solution for poor Rachaya we must hear it,' pleaded Jed.

'Nay, I can't!'

'Shearer,' growled Reg Chandler, grabbing the man by the front of his shirt, 'tell us at once.'

Bale Shearer gulped, a lost man. 'Alright, alright,' he said. Chandler released him. Bale straightened up the front of his shirt. 'In the village of Jh'zak, the closest township to the Impenetrable Mist, they will sometimes have occasion to deal with a witch or someone possessed by demons.'

'What do they do?' asked Jed breathlessly.

'They, ah . . . they tie the offending person to a stake.'

'A stake?'

'A wooden stake, you know, a pyre for fires.' His mouth opened and closed several times. 'They . . . they cleanse the person of evil spirits. They . . . they set them on fire and burn them alive.'

Chandler sat down on his chair with a thud and whistled low. 'That is a heavy price indeed,' he said.

***

Rachaya perched on a stool near her father's workbench. 'Why are you dressing that leg of lamb so nicely?' she asked.

Krishn smiled at her across the table. 'It's Mistress Thatcher's birthday on Rainsday, and she's been good to us – sewing you all those new dresses since you've been growing so much.'

Rachaya smiled fondly. 'I like Mistress Thatcher. She gives Tibbles and me cuts of chicken to eat when we walk past on our way to school.'

'Oh she does, does she?' Krishn laughed. 'That explains your sudden growth spurt, not to mention how fat that cat of yours has grown.'

'Hey! Tibbles is just fluffy.' She looked down at her cat fondly. Tibbles had once belonged to her mother and Rachaya found it difficult to deny the cat treats whenever she begged for them. Her father intercepted the look and shook his head with amusement.

'Mmm, she's especially fluffy around the middle. Now, be useful, Chia, and go fetch me some rosemary for this lamb, will you?'

Rachaya jumped down from the stool and headed outside, her cat trailing along behind her. 'You're not fat, are you girl?' she asked. Tibbles looked out past Rachaya and hissed, her hackles raised.

'Tibbles, what's wrong?' Rachaya turned. There, coming toward them, was a large group of the village's men, each armed with a weapon and an angry expression on his face. Rachaya's stomach lurched with fear – those angry looks were directed at her.

'There she is! The butcher's daughter! Seize her!'

Rachaya let out an ear-piercing scream and ran back toward her father's workshop. At her cry, Krishn came running out to her, colliding with her on the garden path.

'Chia, what is it?' He looked up and saw the men. Fury distorted his face.

'What is the meaning of this?' he shouted. Krishn was a well-built man, more than a match for any of the other villagers. The men eyed Krishn's strong butcher's muscles and hesitated.

Baker stepped out from the mob with his arms extended, palms outward in entreaty. 'We regret the necessity of this, Krishn, but it's the only way. We must stop the demons from taking your daughter.'

Krishn's mouth dropped open. 'Demons? Have you gone mad? All of you?'

'It's because of your wife – Adara. We believe that she sold Rachaya over to demons in exchange for magical powers. She was a witch. That's how she healed young Jed Tanner's leg so well.'

Krishn placed himself in front of his daughter. 'My wife was many things, but a witch was not one of them. Now put down your weapons and leave us in peace!'

Baker shook his head sadly. 'I'm afraid we can't do that, Butcher, not while the safety of Cryll is at stake.'

'Then if you want her you will have to come through me!'

Tibbles growled her agreement and puffed herself out to her full size. Krishn looked down at Rachaya and whispered to her urgently.

'You know that secret signal your mother taught you? To summon her family?'

Rachaya's eyes widened. 'The dragons,' she whispered.

'Yes. Do it. Send the signal. I don't think I'll be able to hold these men off for long.'

Rachaya stared at her father. The dragons? But he had always said that they were dangerous. Why else had her mother fled from them?

The men, frustrated by the delay, cried out. 'Give us your daughter!'

Rachaya's heart hammered in her chest. The dragons may be dangerous, but so were these men. The butcher's daughter clasped the ring on her left hand – golden leaves entwined around a fire-red ruby – and twisted it around her finger three times. The ring grew hotter in her hand, a sign that the signal had worked.

'Krishn, we don't want to hurt you. Just hand over your daughter!'

'Never!' Krishn cried. Rachaya screamed in defiance as the men charged toward them. With muscles powerful from his trade, Krishn knocked men over in twos and threes, but they kept jumping back to their feet. By his side Tibbles fought furiously, an angry ball of fur, biting and scratching at the men. Despite her father's efforts some of the men broke through to Rachaya. She kicked and punched at them with all her might.

She saw her father crumple and fall, Reg Chandler standing over him with a wooden club in his hand.

'No!' she cried. The rest of the men rushed at her and grabbed her. They bound her with rope and shoved a piece of cloth into her mouth. Saul Baker stood before her while another man tied her father up.

'We're truly sorry about this, young Rachaya,' Saul said.

Her whole body trembled and tears welled in her eyes as the men of her village dragged her with them to the centre of town. There she saw what they meant to do with her – the old whipping post, no longer used, was set up with wood and kindling piled up around it. They meant to burn her. With renewed energy borne of fear, Rachaya fought back with every ounce of strength she had left.

It wasn't enough.

CHAPTER 2

THE DRAGON PRINCE

Rachaya struggled against her bonds as the men tied her father securely to the post behind her.

'I'm sorry, Chia,' he groaned. 'I wasn't strong enough.'

Tibbles stood defiantly at their feet, refusing to be moved.

'Leave the stupid cat,' Chandler said. 'It'll scamper as soon as the flames hit.'

'Steady, Reg, we need to explain to the rest of the village first,' Baker said. 'They need to understand why we're doing this.'

A large crowd had gathered around the pyre – almost everyone from the village was there. Through her gag Rachaya screamed with rage. Why was no-one helping them?

Saul Baker stepped forward and raised his hand for silence. The crowd settled, and soon only Rachaya's muffled cries and Tibbles' growls could be heard.

'Today is a sad day in Cryllian history,' he told the waiting crowd. 'It has, to our deepest sorrow, been discovered that the deceased Adara Butcher had engaged in witchcraft. She used this power she gained for good – of that we have no doubt. Young Jed Tanner and his healed leg is a testament to her goodness. But magical powers come from the demons of the Otherworld, and a hefty price must always be paid for any gifts gained.'

The villagers of Cryll broke into an excited babble and Baker had to call them to silence once again.

'As I said, demons never bestow their powers freely and it is our belief that, if they haven't in fact done so already, they mean to redeem their payment in the form of Adara's first-born child.'

As one the crowd gasped and they cried out in unison.

'We must stop them!'

'Demons? Here in Cryll?'

'For mercy's sake, preserve our village!'

'Silence!' Chandler cried out, his wooden club still held aloft. Rachaya continued to fight against her restraints but Chandler had done his job well – they wouldn't budge.

'My daughter is not, nor will ever be, possessed by demons!' roared Krishn, thrashing wildly against his bonds.

'I said *silence*.' Chandler backhanded Krishn across the face.

The villagers quietened, ashen faced and trembling with fear.

'All hope is not lost,' Baker said. 'It just so happens that Bale Shearer was recently visiting the village of Jh'zak, near to the Impenetrable Mist. The villagers there know of a solution to rid themselves of the plague of demons.' He paused, gesturing toward the pyre. 'They must be cleansed with fire.'

At his words a sound, like the rumbling of a stirring volcano, fell upon the villagers' ears from the sky.

'What was that?' Mistress Chandler cried.

'It's the demons! They know we're onto them. They know we mean to stop them. We must hurry!'

A murmur of assent trickled though the gathered villagers. They had to stop the demons, no matter the cost.

'Burn them!' shrieked the crowd. 'Burn them before the demons come!'

But it was too late – a demon had already arrived. With a thunderous roar it fell from the sky, all gleaming yellow scales, talons the size of broadswords with fanged teeth to match, wings held out from its sides like sails, magnificent and glorious.

With a second roar that made the ground shake the beast swooped down and, with a swish of its sinuous tail, knocked the panicked crowd off their feet. Its gleaming maw hovered above the pyre.

I'm going to be eaten, Rachaya thought hysterically as the mouth, its sharp teeth glistening in the sun, descended upon her. The creature's teeth clamped down on the pole she and her father were tied to. The platform was clear now of everyone except Rachaya, Krishn and Tibbles. The beast yanked its enormous head back and launched itself into the air, pulling the pyre, platform and all, clean off the ground. With a thrust of its bat-like wings the creature shot up into the sky and flew away from Cryll, Rachaya and her family dangling precariously from its jaws. The beast flew far, far away, passing villages that looked like toy houses. It covered ground rapidly, flying over farmlands; sheep and cattle were tiny dots of brown and white on the green landscape below. At length it made its descent, dropping the pyre roughly onto the ground of a forest clearing.

Now that they were on the forest floor the dragon didn't seem quite so large. In fact, the creature was *shrinking*. Smaller and smaller it shrunk, the gleaming yellow scales dulled, and the creature took on the form of a human. Standing before them in place of the beast was a red-haired man dressed in elegant, jewel-encrusted clothing that glittered in the dappled sunlight. He looked murderous. He strode over and ripped the gag out of Rachaya's mouth.

'What are you doing with my cousin's ring? Who told you how to send the signal to me?'

Rachaya took quick, shallow breaths and half wished this man would return to his dragon form. He had seemed less scary then.

'Answer me!'

'It was her mother's, given to her freely as a gift,' Krishn said.

The man looked Rachaya up and down, his shrewd blue eyes taking in every detail.

'You do look like her,' he said. He turned to Krishn. 'Adara has a daughter? Where is my cousin? I must see her.'

'My mum died of Boldon fever about three years ago,' Rachaya said.

The stranger ran his fingers through his hair, swearing vehemently. 'No, this cannot be.' Ignoring Rachaya he rounded on Krishn. 'Why didn't you signal me? You obviously knew how.'

'Why would I signal you? She was my *wife*.'

'I could have done something.' The man snarled, looking every inch the dangerous dragon he was before.

'Adara wanted nothing to do with her kind. She was the strongest person I have ever met, and yet she was terrified of meeting with any of your people.'

The man growled and lunged at Krishn. 'My cousin never had cause to fear me. We were as close as brother and sister. You should have signalled me sooner. I should have known about this girl well before now,' he said, gesturing toward Rachaya.

'Why should I have told you?' Krishn said. 'My daughter has nothing to do with you.'

The man brought his face very close to the butcher's. 'Because, *human*,' he said, making it sound like a dirty word, 'your daughter has been left to run amok amongst humans.'

'My daughter does not "run amok".'

'Yes. She. Does. And in doing so she is breaking every single Wizard Law pertaining to dragon kind. She puts us all in grave danger just through her very existence.'

Krishn struggled against his bonds to fight the dragon. 'Adara told me about you – her cousin who would become king of the dragons because she had disappeared without a trace. You may regret my daughter's existence, dragon, but I never will. We want none of your dragons, nor your stupid throne.'

'That's not your choice,' Adara's cousin said quietly. 'You *will* come with me to Fyrebyrne Island. Now, you can do so of your own free will, or I can keep you chained to this pole, a free meal for my dragon friends back home. It's up to you.'

'I would rather die than let you take my daughter.'

'That can be arranged, although it's entirely unnecessary,' the stranger said with a wry smile.

'Why do you want to take us to this island with you?' Rachaya asked.

The dragon turned to her and his expression gentled. 'Your voice even sounds a little like hers, you know.' He shook his head and sighed. 'I knew my cousin well. I know she wouldn't wish me to take you to Fyrebyrne Island with me – she certainly went to enough pains to leave the place. But I must. Duty tells me I must. As soon as the wizards discover your existence they will comb the lands of Escoria in search of you, and they *will* find you. When they do, they will not show you any mercy – the wizards uphold their laws at all costs.' The dragon crouched down before Rachaya so he could look her in the eye.

'But on Fyrebyrne Island, as Crown Princess of the Dragons, you will have a measure of safety that you cannot have here amongst the humans.'

Krishn hung his head in defeat. 'Okay. We will cooperate,' he said.

'Good man,' said the dragon. He untied Rachaya first, then Krishn. Rachaya rubbed her aching arms.

'Where are we?' she asked. 'Are we already on the dragon island?'

Adara's cousin laughed and bent down to pick up Tibbles, who was purring now that the shouting had stopped. 'Goodness, no. If I'd brought humans to Fyrebyrne Island, tied up as you both were, everyone would have assumed I had brought them back a tasty treat. They would have eaten you before I had a chance to say otherwise.'

Rachaya dropped her arms to her sides. 'They'd – they'd eat me? But I'm a dragon. My mother always said I was.'

'Maybe they wouldn't eat you, girl, but they'd certainly eat your father.'

'Then we can't go! Dad, tell him! I will not let you be eaten by dragons!'

The dragon placed his hand on Rachaya's arm. 'Relax, child. I'll keep your father safe.'

'But who are you? How do we know we can trust you?'

The man smiled broadly and shrugged. 'You don't.'

CHAPTER 3

THE SEA OF CERTAIN DEATH

Tibbles was having a wonderful time. The forest was full of birds, you see, and she was convinced she was going to catch every last one of them. It was a shame her travelling companions were not having half as much fun. It all started when the dragon, who called himself Mikel, accused Rachaya and her father of being monsters.

'Why else were your own people planning to kill you?'

'They were convinced demons were going to harm them through possession of my daughter,' retorted Krishn. Rachaya watched the two men open-mouthed – she had never seen grown-ups bicker this way before.

Mikel laughed. 'As if the demons of Azarak would trouble themselves with creatures so weak as humans,' he said.

Krishn bristled. 'I am no weakling.'

'No, maybe not, but you're not as strong as a dragon.'

With a growl that could rival any dragon, Krishn took up the challenge and lunged at Mikel. The two men rolled around on the forest floor, wrestling like schoolboys. Rachaya watched in horror as the prince and the butcher pummelled each other with their fists, grunting like pigs eating swill. Her shouts for them to stop fell on deaf ears and they continued to grapple until they were sweating and covered in leaf litter. Eventually the two men broke apart and climbed to their feet. They were out of breath and, to Rachaya's surprise, smiling. Mikel stepped forward and clapped her father on the shoulder.

'Not a bad effort, Krishn,' he said. 'I can almost see why my cousin chose to marry you.'

Krishn wiped blood from his lip. 'You fought well enough yourself, for a pampered prince.'

Rachaya couldn't believe it. Just like that the two men were friends, even going so far as to brush the dirt off each other. Tibbles came trotting over with a blackbird clamped in her mouth. She dropped it triumphantly at Mikel's feet.

'Nice catch, Tibb—' He stopped and cocked his head to the side as if listening to something. Tibbles meowed at him but he made no other response than to hold a finger to his lips for silence. Without warning he clapped his hands and grinned.

'My friends tell me the passage to Fyrebyrne Island is clear,' he said. 'Are you ready to cross the Sea of Certain Death?'

Rachaya stared up at the dragon with horror. 'The Sea of Certain—'

'Death. That's right.' He smiled widely.

'Why do they call it that?' Her stomach felt like someone was trying to squeeze it through a sieve.

Mikel's eyes widened with delight. 'The sea got its name because any human who makes contact with the water, even in a boat, is certain to drown. Just one of the many tricks the wizards employed to keep us dragons safe.'

Krishn became angry again. 'You promised me I could go to this precious island of yours with my daughter.'

'Relax, Butcher. I'm a dragon of my word. You will be travelling in royal style – on the back of a glorious dragon.'

'But why do dragons need wizards to protect them?' Rachaya asked. 'They're *dragons*.'

Mikel shrugged. 'I guess you could say dragons and humans haven't always seen eye-to-eye.'

'If all dragons are like you then I can see why,' Krishn said.

Mikel held his hands up in surrender. 'Okay, okay. We called a truce and I will honour it. Now, are you two ready? My friends are not exactly the most patient of dragons.'

Before they could say anything more Mikel's face began to twist and distort. His eyes turned from blue to a brilliant emerald green. His nose elongated into a snout and his teeth became dangerously long and sharp. Up and out the dragon grew until Rachaya had to crane her neck to look up at him. Mikel's skin turned into scales that looked diamond-hard, yellow and lustrous. Enormous wings erupted from his shoulderblades, and a swishing tale grew out from behind. Rachaya caught her breath.

He was majestic.

With a grace that only a cat could manage, Tibbles scaled the prince's foreleg and snuggled down above his shoulder. Mikel snapped his powerful jaws playfully at Rachaya and her father.

'You go first,' Rachaya told her father. 'It's me he wants. I don't want to risk him leaving you behind.'

Krishn nodded, his jaw set firm. 'I'll see you up there.'

Rachaya watched as her father climbed up the side of the dragon, gripping tightly onto Mikel's scales. As she waited her turn she was struck by a terrifyingly terrific thought – one day she might be able to transform into a dragon. A thrill of excitement rippled through her body. Perhaps something good would come out of this terrible day after all.

Krishn, meanwhile, had made his way to the base of the dragon's neck next to Tibbles.

'Come on, Chia,' he called.

Rachaya gripped between the grooves of two of Mikel's hard scales and pulled herself up off the ground. It was more difficult than Tibbles and Krishn had made it look. The scales were as smooth as gemstones and just as slippery. Muscles in her fingers cried out with pain, muscles she had never known existed before now. Bit by bit she climbed, sweat making her ascent even more of a challenge. Finally, she was hoisted up the rest of the way by her father and was seated in front of him.

'Hold on to the scales,' Krishn instructed.

Rachaya took hold just as Mikel raised his glorious wings high in the air until the tips were touching. Then, with a downward thrust, he launched into the sky. They continued to steadily rise until they were high above the swaying treetops. The motion of the dragon's wings changed slightly and they were suddenly propelled forward.

This was much better than being carried through the air while chained to a wooden post.

This was exhilarating!

Rachaya let out a whoop of joy as they soared through the air, the landscape flashing past them in a blur of blues, greens and browns. Her worries from the day blew away from her in the wind and she gave herself to the sheer delight of the moment.

Far off in the distance a glittering ocean began to appear – the Sea of Certain Death. How could anything so beautiful be so dangerous? The water was calm, with only the tiniest of ripples disturbing its surface.

Mikel began to zoom even faster through the sky and loose strands of hair whipped about Rachaya's face in a frenzy. She reached up to remove them from her eyes.

'Don't let go!' cried her father, clamping down hard on her waist in a vice-like grip. Rachaya took hold of the dragon's scales and smiled to herself. It looked like her father was more afraid than he was trying to let on.

Through squinted eyes she looked out ahead. There before them, among the sparkling grey water, sat a dark speck of land. As they drew nearer, the tiny speck transformed itself into a large island, complete with ragged cliffs and lush greenery. It grew before their very eyes and, before too long, Mikel began to make his descent. Krishn's grip on Rachaya grew even tighter and he began to curse horribly under his breath. The dragon dropped his wings to his sides and let himself freefall. The ground rushed up at Rachaya and she could see every pebble, every blade of grass, as distinctly as she could see the dragon's yellow scales on his neck. For the first time since climbing aboard the dragon she felt true fear. Her screams intermingled with those from her father. Just as she was certain their bodies were going to colour the grass with their splattered remains, Mikel pulled up and made a smooth, well-practised landing.

With a thundering roar the dragon reared up on his hind legs, throwing Rachaya and her companions unceremoniously onto the spongy grass. By the time he had transformed back into his human body, tears of laughter were streaming down his face.

Rachaya launched herself to her feet, her hands balled into fists at her side. She had expected that her father would be right there beside her, yelling at this devilish dragon. Instead he was bent over being heartily sick, his face as green as the grass they had been dumped upon. Mikel was far from threatened by the girl – he was doubled over with laughter now, clutching at his sides. Rachaya stormed over and pushed him on the shoulder.

'Hey!' he said. 'Oh, come now. That was funny!'

She opened her mouth to respond but the ground began to rumble beneath her feet, halting her mid-yell. The island began to groan and shake as a gathering cloud of dust made its way toward them. The prince wiped the tears from his face and tidied his clothes, unperturbed by the commotion.

'I hope you're both ready,' he said.

Three hulking monsters skidded to a halt before them, scattering dirt into their faces.

'Now the fun really begins.'

CHAPTER 4

A THING OR TWO ABOUT DRAGONS

Rachaya looked around desperately for somewhere to hide, but there was no escape from these monsters. They were as unlike Mikel as it was possible to be, and yet they were still quite patently dragons. Their heads were broad and flat with two lethal horns perched on top. Their dark shoulders were round and muscled, not sleek and smooth like Mikel's. Where the prince had wings, these beasts had steel-like plates that snaked across their shoulders and down their sides. Their scales were smoother, more intricately linked together. Out of the end of each foot grew talons that were the stuff of nightmares – broad, long and strong, like that of a wombat. These were creatures equipped with many options for killing a person quickly. Rachaya felt relieved when the beasts began to transform, until she saw what they looked like in human form. The trio were just as well muscled in their human bodies, each easily twice the size of Rachaya's father. If looks could kill, Rachaya and her companions would have withered and died on the spot.

The biggest and meanest looking of the bunch drew a sword from its scabbard and held it to Mikel's throat. 'You told us you were going to retrieve Princess Adara,' he growled.

Rachaya thought she was going to wet herself, but the prince remained calm.

'I had believed at the time that I would,' he said.

'But instead you brought humans. *Humans*, Mikel. What is the meaning of this?'

Krishn stood up taller – he was not going to be weighed down by insults thrown from the mouths of dragons.

Mikel reached out and pushed the sword away from his throat. 'It's all above board, Ardhan, I can assure you. I have not broken my word to the earth dragons.'

One of Ardhan's companions stepped forward.

'You had best explain yourself, Prince, and fast, because from here it looks like you've been lying to us.'

Mikel ignored the dragon and turned his focus back to Ardhan, whose muscles were bulging threateningly beneath his dark skin.

'When Adara and I were children we had a secret way of signalling each other. I received a signal just like it today,' Mikel said. 'However, it was not my cousin, but her daughter who sent the call.'

Ardhan scowled at Rachaya and looked her up and down. 'And the human?'

'Adara's husband and Princess Rachaya's father.'

Ardhan rounded on Mikel again, this time clutching him by the throat. 'Adara would never mate with a *human*,' he spat.

Mikel's eyes rapidly changed from blue to emerald green and the earth dragon dropped his hands from the prince's throat. Blisters bubbled on Ardhan's hands and fingers. He growled but made no further move toward the prince. The earth dragon turned his attention back to Rachaya instead, ignoring his injuries.

'She does look like Adara,' he said.

'Enough of this,' said the second of Ardhan's companions. 'Where's Princess Adara?'

'Dead,' said Rachaya before she could stop herself. She forced herself to stand up straighter, just as she had seen her father do. All three earth dragons stared at her with disbelief.

'She died of the Boldon fever three years ago,' she said.

Ardhan staggered backward as if he had been struck. 'No, this cannot be. Not Adara. She was our only hope.'

Mikel gripped the earth dragon by the arm. 'She left us with a gift – a daughter,' he said quietly. 'Don't give up the fight just yet.'

'But she's human—'

'She's a dragon. Adara was certain of it. My cousin would never have given her the heir's ring if it were not so.'

Ardhan focused on the ring on Rachaya's finger. Anger receded from his face, replaced instead with worry. 'Mikel, your journey today took you to *Escoria*. Think of what the wizards will do if they find out Adara raised her daughter there.'

Rachaya felt a thrill of fear creep its way up her spine. What was it about the wizards that made mighty dragons speak of them with such dread?

'I know what the wizards will want to do and we must stop them,' Mikel said. 'For that we need time to set Rachaya up as the official Crown Princess.'

A silent message passed between Mikel and the earth dragons.

Ardhan nodded. 'We will buy you time,' he said. He turned to Rachaya and bowed. 'Princess Rachaya and human-father, we welcome you to Fyrebyrne Island – for welcome you we must, if you are to avoid being eaten,' he said to Krishn.

The enormous man then turned back to the prince and spoke with surprising gentleness. 'You can count on us, Mikel. But you must also do whatever you can to keep this girl safe – from everyone.'

'I will see to it that she faces no danger,' Mikel replied. Ardhan signalled to the other two earth dragons, who had dropped back respectfully during the conversation. With a wave to Mikel they transformed back into colossal beasts and ran toward the heart of the island, a trail of dust rising in their wake.

'Earth dragons,' Mikel said with a little shake of his head. 'Unpredictable tempers, but they're loyal where it's deserved.'

'I'm just glad they didn't eat me,' Krishn said, his shoulders relaxing a little.

'I told you you'd be safe with me. Now, come. We must make haste.'

Mikel started walking further inland and the others followed him. Tibbles darted off every now and then to chase a fly or bee, but otherwise stayed close.

The terrifying image of gigantic earth dragons left a lasting imprint on Rachaya's mind. Although she had always known that dragons existed – had always known that she was a dragon herself – coming face-to-face with them was an entirely different experience.

'Are earth dragons always so angry?' she asked.

Mikel laughed. 'Yes, they're renowned for it,' he said.

'But they look so different to you. What kind of dragon are you?'

'I'm a fire dragon, as was your mother – as are you.'

Rachaya nodded and, before she could change her mind, asked the question that was really bothering her.

'What will the wizards want to do to me?'

Krishn put an arm around her shoulders for comfort. Her father seemed to already know Mikel's answer.

'As a dragon you are not allowed to live anywhere other than Fyrebyrne Island until you have graduated from school,' Mikel said.

'But I wasn't even born here.'

'That won't alter Wizard Law in the slightest.'

'Chia, the punishment is death,' said Krishn quietly. 'I'm so sorry. That's why your mother and I kept you a secret from the dragons for so long.'

Rachaya pulled away from her father. 'You knew this and yet you let a dragon bring me here?'

'Your father did the right thing,' Mikel said. 'In Escoria the wizards could do whatever they liked to you and no-one would ever know. In bringing you out into the open we have forced their hand – they will be accountable for their actions. They will have to be careful. And if we're lucky we may just be able to make their own laws work against them.'

'But their laws state that they can kill me.' Panic blurred her vision and she forced herself to fight against it.

'No, they can't. Not just like that,' Mikel said gently.

Krishn reached out and put his arm back around her shoulder, giving her a hug. 'You know what your mother would say, Chia. Don't get up out of your seat to greet trouble just yet. Wait until it has started knocking on your front door.' Her father seemed so calm that she allowed herself to calm, too. There was no point dwelling on possible trouble in the future.

'Tell me about the other dragon types,' she said. 'Are there just fire and earth dragons?'

Mikel shuddered dramatically. 'No, thank goodness. We'd tear each other to pieces if not for the peace-keeping races.'

Krishn laughed at the surprised look on Rachaya's face. 'What he's trying to say is that not all dragons have such awful tempers. Your mother was always sure to tell me so whenever I blamed her fiery temper on the fact that she was a dragon. "Not all dragons have tempers," she'd say. "That's what makes me so special."'

Rachaya chuckled. She could well imagine her mother saying something like that.

'Adara was always proud of her fierce spirit,' said Mikel. 'She would have made an excellent warrior queen.' For a brief moment Mikel's face betrayed some of his grief, but he covered it quickly with a smile. 'What with the fiery fire dragons and egregious earth dragons, it seems only right that we also have winsome water dragons, too,' he said.

'What are these other dragons like? Are they big, like Ardhan?'

'Thankfully not. Water dragons don't have much by way of muscle. Instead they are covered with essential blubber to keep them warm in their subaquatic habitat. Like earth dragons they lack true wings. Instead, water dragons have small stubs that act like oars.'

'And they keep the peace between earth and fire dragons?'

'With the help of tiny air dragons, yes. But don't be fooled by their diminutive stature. Air dragons have ways of halting even the most ferocious of fights. What is more they can fly as swiftly as any eagle.'

'I had no idea there'd be four different types of dragons. I imagined they'd all be like my mum.'

'No, there are five types,' Krishn said. 'Just you wait until Mikel tells you about the sun dragons.'

Rachaya looked up expectantly at Mikel. To her surprise he wasn't smiling.

'Oh come now, Butcher, sun dragons are nothing but a myth,' he said. 'I have no idea why Adara would even mention them to you.'

'Because they sound incredible,' replied Krishn. 'Chia, they were meant to be bigger than all the other races of dragons combined. Their magic rivalled the power of the sun. Doesn't that make all the other dragons sound about as harmless as Tibbles?'

'Ah, now I see,' said Mikel, a smile returning to his face. 'You tell yourself there's an even scarier dragon than me so you can sleep easier at night.' The dragon shrugged his shoulders with princely grace. 'I guess I can allow that.'

Rachaya could feel her father tense beside her, ready to pounce on the prince.

'Look at that,' she said to distract him, pointing randomly in the distance.

Mikel beamed with pride. 'Marvellous, isn't it? Butcher, Rachaya, welcome to your new home. I present to you Perfero Castle.'

CHAPTER 5

A NEW HEIR TO THE DRAGON THRONE

With Mikel in the lead the group drew closer to Perfero Castle. Soon they had to crane their necks to look up at it. The castle itself was enveloped in a towered curtain wall, which was tall enough to block the castle grounds from view, but not nearly big enough to hide the enormity of the structure within. Atop the wall, at regular intervals, stood several multicoloured flags fluttering merrily in the breeze. Their movement mimicked that of Rachaya's stomach as they neared her new home.

Perfero Castle itself rose high above the landscape. Its four towers had been carved from glittering black granite, elegant and smooth. An array of colourful jewels was embedded in the stone. Even from a distance, Rachaya could see that each gem – every emerald, ruby and sapphire – was bigger than her fist. Suddenly Mikel's jewel-encrusted clothing made more sense as a fashion statement than it had in Escoria.

They crossed a wide moat coated with algal blooms and lily pads and walked up to the intimidating front gate. There, standing to attention, were two dragons in human form guarding the castle entrance. The guard on the left was definitely an earth dragon. Rachaya was sure she could see his muscles even beneath his armour. But the second guard was, she suspected, a water dragon, complete with a round belly which looked like it was made of blubber. With one neat sidestep the two dragons blocked the group's entrance to the castle grounds.

'Meaning no disrespect, Prince Mikel, sir, but we've received no orders that you'd be bringing strangers to the castle,' said the water dragon, his grey eyes wide with concern.

The earth dragon growled and started sniffing the air like a hound. 'You've brought *humans*,' he said. 'Dinner for the king's birthday feast next month, maybe?' He leered at Krishn, licking his lips.

Mikel drew himself to his full height, his eyes once again changing colour.

'This man is here as my guest and is *not* to be eaten,' he said. 'Any dragon who touches so much as a hair on his head shall answer directly to me.' He stared down the two guards, never taking his eyes off them until they looked away in submission.

'As to the identities of my guests, that is my concern and mine alone; I am answerable to no-one but the king. Now stand aside and let us pass in peace.'

The water dragon sprang aside instantly, his stomach swaying from side to side from the motion.

'No disrespect intended, my lord, no disrespect,' he said, his pudgy arm raised in a salute. The earth dragon begrudgingly stepped aside, too, his half-hearted salute doing nothing to hide his scowl. Mikel marched through the gates with Rachaya, Krishn and Tibbles in his wake.

'First rule of ruling,' he said to Rachaya. 'Never explain your decisions to your subordinates. Be polite, be respectful, but never grant them the power of laying judgement on your decisions.'

'I don't want to rule,' Rachaya said quietly.

'No-one wants to rule, not really. But rule you must, and you need to learn how to do it well. You cannot fight your inheritance.'

Mikel stopped his companions once they reached the courtyard and threw his arms out wide. 'Just take a look around you,' he said. 'I love coming home to this. Isn't it glorious?'

The castle's courtyard was so large that as many as ten Mikel-sized dragons could walk around it with plenty of room to stretch their wings. The castle itself consisted of three separate parts – the left wing, centre wing and right wing. Each section had flagstone steps leading up to a golden door. Arching above each door were careful carvings of men, women, children and forest creatures. Prominent of all were etchings of dragons, in all their glory. Rachaya could have admired the carvings for days on end, but Mikel didn't give her any time to loiter. He ushered his companions up the steps and through the golden doors.

Inside was more magnificent, more majestic than the castle's exterior. The very sight caused Rachaya to stop dead in her tracks. Krishn slammed into the back of her, sending her sprawling across the polished parquetry floor. She blushed furiously when several castle guards came running over to discover the cause of the commotion. Mikel spoke with the guards and, avoiding their curious gazes, Rachaya took the opportunity to discreetly climb to her feet and look around her. The vast walls were covered with silk tapestries, the needlework so fine the subjects looked like they could come to life. Strips of luxurious carpet lined the walkways, trailing up the sweeping staircase to the upper floors. Glittering chandeliers dangled from the lofty ceiling, scattering light around the chamber like fireflies.

Rachaya didn't think she would ever get used to such opulence, nor the idea of being the ruler of dragons.

Krishn brushed off Rachaya's skirt and helped steady her. The guards, having been appropriately dealt with, returned to their posts. Mikel led them up the stairs and along equally well-decorated corridors.

The journey was a long one but eventually they arrived at their destination. Mikel halted before an enormous set of oaken doors that towered menacingly above them. Dragons made of invaluable gemstones patterned the door, fiercely guarding the chamber that lay within.

'We are about to go in and greet the king,' Mikel said in an urgent whisper. 'Everything hinges upon this meeting going well. Be polite. Be respectful. Bow down as low as you can possibly go. But most importantly, let me do most of the talking. I have learnt how to read the king's moods.'

Without waiting for them to respond Mikel threw open the doors and swept into the expansive audience chamber. He bowed down before an elderly dragon with stark white hair. Rachaya and her father copied the prince's fluid movements as best they could; Tibbles marched in and stared balefully up at the king, as irreverent as ever.

'By my own eyes I can see my beautiful daughter . . . and yet Adara should be older than this, a grown woman in truth.' The king turned uncertainly to Mikel. 'Nephew, what is this new sorcery?'

'Your majesty, I beg leave of you to explain myself free from any interruptions.'

The king nodded and waved a withered hand to the guards. They moved in front of the door, preventing any further guests from entering the chamber.

'Explain this mirage to me, Mikel. What I see before me troubles my ageing eyes greatly.'

Mikel knelt down before the king. 'Your highness, through a stroke of good fortune I stumbled across a village in Escoria who knew of our dear Adara. They knew her well – they loved her well, I believe. But I was too late.' The prince bowed his head and spoke to the floor. 'Princess Adara died three years ago of the Boldon fever.'

The king threw himself backward on his throne in disbelief. 'A fire dragon dying of a fever? Preposterous!'

Mikel looked up at him imploringly. 'My lord, it breaks my heart to contradict, but it is the truth.' He reached out and took the king's hand. 'Even dead, Adara has done us well, my liege. She did her duty to the family. She married this man standing here before you and together they had a child. Adara gave you a legitimate heir to the dragon throne.' He climbed to his feet and stood beside Rachaya. The king sat perfectly still.

'My king, this girl I have brought before you today is Rachaya Butcher Perfero, Crown Princess of the Dragons.'

The king rose from his golden throne and gazed upon Rachaya's face.

'An heir,' he breathed. 'And with such a name. Many of our greatest queens were called Rachaya.' The old man's face lit up with delight, but his excitement gave way immediately to despair. 'Nephew, where did you say you found the village Adara had lived in?'

'It is as you fear, my lord. I found Princess Rachaya and her father living in the human world; they were indeed inhabitants of Escoria.'

The king's face turned beet red and tiny flames sparked from his fingertips. 'But it is forbidden! The law! It must be obeyed!' He swung around violently and faced Rachaya. 'Girl. Have you naturalised yet?'

Rachaya was stunned. 'Have I what?'

'Naturalised, child! Have you claimed your birthright – have you grown into your dragon skin?'

'The king is asking if you have transformed into your dragon body yet,' Mikel said.

Rachaya's heart sank. She was going to disappoint them before her first day on Fyrebyrne Island had ended. She wasn't enough of a dragon.

'No,' she admitted. 'I haven't made the change yet.'

To her surprise, the king and Mikel seemed relieved to hear it.

'In that case, Princess, you might just stand a chance,' the king said. He held a hand up to Rachaya's face.

'My girl's eyes were the blue of a summer's day,' he said. 'Your eyes may be brown but I can see that you are a true granddaughter of mine.' He removed his hand and returned to his throne.

'Mikel, how long do you think we'll have before the wizards arrive?'

'A day. Maybe two if we're lucky.'

'Then we must act with all haste and pray that we are lucky. Consult with Aja, get him to prepare a coronation ceremony for the heir apparent.' The king looked at Mikel with embarrassment. 'I'm sorry, nephew, it's a necessity—'

'It's okay, Uncle. I willingly relinquish the crown to Adara's child.'

'You're a good dragon, nephew. You do your duty well. Make the preparations and ensure Princess Rachaya and her father are housed with all possible comforts.'

Mikel bowed to the king and gestured for the others to follow him from the room. Krishn's arm fell on Rachaya's shoulder as the enormous oak doors closed behind them.

'Everything's going to be okay, Chia,' he whispered.

Mikel rubbed his hands together and smiled at his companions.

'Well, that went better than I expected,' he said. 'Now for the fun part: informing my wife and child that we have a new heir to the dragon throne.' An expression of concern flitted across his face.

'I take it your family won't be happy,' Krishn said, mirroring his daughter's thoughts.

Mikel smiled. 'I am certain that they will be most displeased,' he said. He shot Krishn a wicked grin. 'Rest assured, my friend, I'll do my very best to prevent them from eating you.'

CHAPTER 6

LADY ANJELA IS NOT IMPRESSED

'Come and rest in my apartments first,' said Mikel. 'Both of you must be exhausted by now. You may as well be comfortable while the servants prepare a room for you.'

Rachaya heaved a sigh of relief and eagerly followed Mikel. The last of her energy had failed her a long time ago and she was feeling light-headed and woozy. Looking across at her father's wan face, she could see that he wasn't feeling the best, either.

Mikel led them through yet another labyrinth of corridors. Rachaya felt certain she would never be able to find her way around Perfero Castle by herself – in fact, it was a good thing the place was crawling with servants who would be able to point her in the right direction.

There was nothing special about the door leading to Mikel's apartments. It looked exactly the same as the hundreds they had passed on the way. But inside was as highly decorative as the dragon himself. Gemstones were worked into every piece of furniture, every wall fixture; even the curtains sparkled with tiny diamonds. The sitting room was enormous. Mikel would have had no trouble transforming in here. Rachaya and her father gratefully sat down on the comfortable sofa at the far end of the room, right next to the fireplace. It felt good to take the weight off her shaking legs.

'Will you two be alright if I leave you here while I go and organise your rooms?' Mikel asked.

Rachaya and Krishn nodded wearily – now that they were seated, neither of them were keen to stand up again anytime soon.

'Excellent. I'll see about having some food brought up for you, too. And, ah . . . if a blond woman comes in – you'll know who I mean when you see her – send a signal to me with the ring again. Although, it's best no-one else around here knows what the ring can do, so try to be subtle.'

Mikel left them to the peace and quiet, the crackling fire in the grate the only sound in the room. Tibbles jumped up onto Rachaya's lap and made herself comfortable. She was lovely and warm, and her purrs were soothing. The new princess lay her head on her father's sturdy shoulder and closed her stinging eyes. She let her guard down and began to doze.

Rachaya fell into a strange dream. She was watching a handful of dragons punch a large ball up into the air, knocking it back and forth to each other with their snouts. The rhythmic movements relaxed her until it dawned on her: *she* was the ball being hit back and forth. She struggled to break free.

Rachaya jerked awake to the sound of raised voices coming from behind the sitting-room door. She thought she recognised Mikel's cultured voice.

'Anjela,' the man who sounded like Mikel was saying, 'you need to calm down.'

'No, I do *not*. I have every right to be as angry as it is possible to be!'

This was followed by a loud thud, as if someone had hit the wooden door with a clenched fist.

'You have plucked the crown from atop my head and placed it on a girl that you didn't even know existed until today. And you expect me to be *happy* about that?'

Another thud. Rachaya and her father exchanged worried glances. Should they go out and try to help him? They heard the prince respond in a calm voice, but they couldn't quite catch his words.

'Mikel, Adara ran off and abandoned her people. She left you behind to pick up the pieces. Think of all the sacrifices you have had to make. Are you really going to give everything up just because your cousin had a daughter?'

'Yes, I am.'

'What of our son?'

'What of him?' Steel crept into Mikel's voice, giving it a dangerous edge.

'You are stealing the crown from our beautiful boy's innocent fingers!'

'The crown was never truly his, nor was it ever truly yours. The both of you will do well enough without it.'

Another thud sounded, but this time the door flew open with it, creaking on its hinges. Standing in the doorway was a well-dressed blond woman with a savage expression on her thin face.

'So *this* is her then? This is the girl you would give everything up for?' She huffed in disgust. 'Why, there's nothing to her. She's not even pretty.'

Rachaya leapt to her feet. Her father grabbed her around the waist and yanked her back onto the sofa. Tibbles meowed her displeasure at having been thrown to the floor.

'And you brought that awful creature back with you.' The woman wrinkled up her nose in distaste. 'You seem determined to upset me today, Mikel. I'm sure I don't know what I've done to deserve it.' She looked Rachaya and Krishn up and down, hatred and disdain radiating from her face like smouldering coals in a fire pit.

'I will not let this go lightly, Mikel,' she said. 'I will fight you with everything I have over this.'

With those parting words she stalked from the room.

'Oh dear,' said Mikel, but the cheeky grin on his face said that he wasn't even remotely sorrowful. He closed the door and sat down.

'So that was my wife, Lady Anjela,' he said. 'She seems to have forgotten her manners today, but I can assure you she comes from an excellent pedigree.'

'She isn't the sort of person I had imagined you would be married to,' Rachaya blurted out.

Mikel laughed. 'You speak the truth, Rachaya, but I would caution you to guard your tongue more closely now that you are amongst dragons.' He reached out and picked the cat up. 'A prince does not often get to choose his bride for himself.'

Mikel stroked the cat and stretched out his long legs. 'I have not been idle while I have been away,' he said. 'I have spoken with all the right advisers and have managed to set your coronation for this evening. I have also managed to wrangle some apartments for you both. Adara's old rooms are being readied for you as we speak.'

Krishn leant forward and held out his hand for the dragon to shake. 'Thank you, Mikel. For everything. Today you have saved our lives more times than I am sure we are aware of.'

'You have given us so much,' said Rachaya.

Mikel brushed their thanks aside. 'Nonsense. I have given you nothing that wasn't already yours by right.'

'But your wife . . .'

Mikel shrugged. 'It's not as if we will be left destitute. Besides, I never wanted to be king. I was raised to support the ruler, not to actually rule myself. My wife wed me knowing that. She is no innocent maiden; she knows where things stand.'

A tiny dragon entered the room. She stood about as tall as Rachaya's waist, and yet she was quite definitely an adult.

'Princess Adara's suite is ready for accommodation,' the dragon announced before scurrying from the room.

'Air dragons,' said Mikel with a happy smile. 'They're very efficient. Just don't expect them to hang around for any further instructions.'

Adara's rooms were a surprise to Rachaya. They were far more relaxed than Mikel's, with none of the gemstones and jewels that the prince seemed to favour. The furniture was elegant yet comfortable, in natural wood tones and soft creams. Rachaya immediately fell in love with the place.

'I suggest you both get some sleep,' Mikel said. 'A coronation is a tedious ceremony at best and an exhausting one at worst.'

He left them to explore their new home. As soon as he was gone Krishn whistled softly.

'What a day, hey Chia?'

'You can say that again,' she replied. They wandered across the room to a simple oak door at the other end. Behind it lay a lovely bed chamber, with an enormous four-poster bed in pride of place. Its green curtains matched the hangings in front of the window. A woman's dresser sat opposite with an oval mirror propped above it. Candles were scattered around the room and it felt cosy and safe.

Rachaya sat down on the edge of the bed and took her boots off.

'Dad?' she said.

'Mmm?'

'Aren't you worried the dragons will try to eat you?'

Krishn snorted. 'Nah, they all look well fed enough, don't you think? Besides, if I could handle your mother I can handle any dragon. Now, it's time you got some proper sleep.'

Rachaya climbed into the voluminous bed and pulled the blankets up to her chin.

'Do you think we will be happy here?' she asked. Krishn stroked her hair back from her face.

'Of course we'll be happy. You're home now, Chia, and we're here together. We can ask for nothing more.'

He kissed her forehead and turned to leave. Rachaya was so tired she was asleep before he had reached the door.

***

Rachaya was pulled from a deep slumber thanks to a bright light that was shining onto her face. Her father had returned, carrying a candle with him. Night-time had fallen in earnest while she had slept.

'It's time to get up, Chia. Mikel says all is ready for your coronation.'

Rachaya had been so exhausted she hadn't given the coronation ceremony a second thought. Now that it was here it felt as if a dozen air dragons were jumping up and down in her belly.

'Do I really have to do this?' she asked.

Krishn sat down on the edge of the bed and placed the candle on the nightstand. 'Yes, I'm afraid you do,' he said gently. 'I've spoken with Mikel about it further and he thinks it's essential. We need to do everything we can to make sure the wizards can't hurt you. If making you the heir apparent will save your life, then that's what we need to do.'

'But I'll – I'll be queen one day.'

'And a damn good one, too, if I know my little girl at all. Now get up and make yourself presentable. We don't want to present the dragons with a shabby princess.'

Krishn braided Rachaya's hair for her, just like he used to do when she was little. Mikel had brought her a sumptuous silk dress and some emeralds for her throat. She looked older and very much like the princesses of her imagination. Her father beamed at her proudly, holding an arm out for her to take.

'Come on then, Princess Rachaya,' he said. 'Let's show these dragons what a daughter of Adara and Krishn Butcher can do.'

Rachaya allowed herself to be led out of the safety of her mother's rooms and into the dragon's den.

CHAPTER 7

HEAD WIZARD MATHONWY IS NOT IMPRESSED

Rachaya was feeling very proud of herself. She was actually recognising features within the castle that gave her an idea of where she was heading. The distinctive jewelled dragons on the enormous oak doors loomed ahead of her, telling her that she was approaching the king's audience chamber. But just when she thought she knew where she was going, Mikel took her through a small side door she hadn't noticed before. A bevy of servants awaited her arrival in the small antechamber. The second they saw her they leapt into action. The dragons bustled around her, covering her with clothing fit for a dragon queen. They placed a warrior's chest plate over her silk gown. It was made of pure gold and felt uncomfortably heavy. Around her waist they wound a wide leather belt, studded with rubies and sapphires. A heavy sword dangled from the belt, sheathed in an ornate scabbard. Over her shoulders they threw a cape of soft, silken fur. With much clucking and readjusting, Rachaya was finally deemed ready for the coronation ceremony.

'Kneel down before the king and he'll do the rest,' said Mikel, taking her to stand before the intimidating audience chamber doors. This time they didn't just barge into the room, throwing open the doors. Instead they waited, Rachaya resisting the urge to fiddle with her new clothes.

Mikel smiled and winked at Rachaya when trumpets sounded from within the chamber.

'They're ready for us,' he said. The doors were opened for them by a pair of water dragons, their armour polished to perfection in honour of the occasion.

Rachaya held herself upright under the crushing weight of the armour. She nearly slumped down in defeat when she saw how many dragons were in the room to witness her coronation. There were tiny air dragons standing on tiptoe, craning their necks to try to see beyond the bulky water dragons. Earth dragons stood in knots around the room, with fire dragons interspersed throughout the crowd. Each dragon was covered head to toe in priceless jewellery. They looked up at Rachaya expectantly. The new princess forced herself to remain poised, and she managed to walk into the room at a measured pace. She hoped she looked as regal as Mikel did; she suspected she looked like a child draped in her mother's too-big clothing, playing at dress-ups.

The dragons began chattering excitedly, sounding like the birds Tibbles had been chasing in the forest earlier that the day. Doing her best to shut out the sound, Rachaya knelt down before the elderly king and bowed her head respectfully.

A hush descended upon the chamber as the king rose to his feet and stepped down to stand before his granddaughter's prostrate form. Her neck itched under the gaze of hundreds of pairs of avidly watching eyes. The king drew his sword and Rachaya felt a moment of panic when she saw it glitter in the candlelight. He merely held it flat out before her.

'Princess Rachaya Butcher Perfero,' the king said, 'place your hands upon the sword.'

She followed the king's command, hoping no-one noticed her shaking hands. She kept her head lowered, thinking she might lose her nerve if she looked him in the eyes.

The king raised his voice so the entire audience chamber could hear. 'To be a good leader of dragons one must be strong. One must be willing and able to defend one's people with all of one's strength. To be queen one must serve one's dragons with her every waking breath. She must rule justly; she must rule wisely and with a noble heart.'

The king reached out with his free hand and tilted Rachaya's chin so that she was looking up at him.

'Rachaya Butcher Perfero, *legitimate* daughter of Adara Perfero, granddaughter of King Stimeon Perfero – you have been measured and you have been found worthy to be our rightful heir, to take upon thine shoulders the mantle of Crown Princess, to one day rule as Queen of the Dragons. Do you accept this burden, as you accept this privilege?'

The king's icy-blue eyes looked kindly upon Rachaya. He smiled ever so slightly, offering her what little encouragement he could in such a public space. She felt her confidence grow.

'I do,' she managed to reply, her voice coming out in a croak.

'Then rise, Rachaya, Crown Princess of the Dragons!'

The Crown Princess rose to her quivering feet. The gathered crowd erupted into enthusiastic applause. The king moved Rachaya so she was standing beside him. Mikel came to stand on the other side of the king, beaming his approval to the crowd. Rachaya smiled with relief. Her mother's people were accepting her.

The moment was short lived.

The audience-chamber doors burst open with a thundering crash that was heard clearly over the raucous cheering of the dragons. The audience halted mid-applause. Standing in the doorway was a triumphant Lady Anjela. She strode into the room with the grace of a lioness. Following close behind her was a red-haired boy of around fifteen or sixteen. An elderly man entered after them. He was most definitely not a dragon; he had a long, bushy beard that reached down to his waist, a tall pointed hat with a wide brim, and flowing crimson robes. The very sight of this man made Mikel's skin begin to radiate heat, warming Rachaya's face even from this distance. She looked over at him and saw his eyes were glowing emerald green. The prince stepped forward, his hand resting on the hilt of his ceremonial sword.

'Why, my good wife, you have arrived too late for the coronation ceremony. But we would be honoured if you will join the family up here on the dais – my son, too – so that you can offer your congratulations to the new Crown Princess.'

Lady Anjela's eyes flashed from her usual blue to red at the news that she had not arrived in time to halt proceedings. Before she could speak the bearded man strode forward. His black eyes glittered with anger.

'We cannot come forward with a spirit of celebration when a heinous crime has been committed – a crime of such magnitude that it must be addressed at once.'

The king gaped at the man like a buffoon. Mikel, however, was not to be intimidated.

'We know of no crime, Head Wizard Mathonwy. The ceremony was performed to the very letter of the law.'

The wizard's beard bristled with indignation. 'Do not play the fool with me, dragon. I have it on very good authority that your newly found Crown Princess has, in fact, been residing in Escoria despite being underage.'

The crowd gasped, fixing Rachaya with a scandalised gaze that was not half as friendly as it had been before.

'Where the princess was born is no fault of her own,' said Mikel.

'And yet it is so often the children who must pay for the sins of their fathers,' Lady Anjela said. Rachaya wanted to slap the smug look from her angular face.

'Prince Mikel, we choose to believe that you have brought the princess here in good faith, fully adhering to the law. Your wife has assured us that it was always your intention to hand the offender over to the Wizard Assembly so that justice can be done.' The wizard smiled, but his crooked yellow teeth looked more like they were forming a snarl than a friendly gesture. 'When this dragon has been found guilty we shall happily restore you and your family as heirs to the dragon throne.'

Mikel drew his sword. '*When* she's found guilty? Begging your pardon, Head Wizard, but I had always believed that the wizards were just; that they believed in a fair and honest trial for all peoples.' He stepped sideways so he was blocking Rachaya from the wizard's view. 'A member of royalty cannot simply be arrested, Mathonwy. You can summon the Crown Princess to trial. Anything further would be overextending the arm of the law.'

The wizard reached into the folds of his voluminous robes and pulled out a roll of parchment. He marched up to Rachaya, leant around Mikel, and thrust the document into her hands.

'The Wizard Assembly always has, and always will, uphold the law. With deep regret we summon the fire dragon, Crown Princess Rachaya Butcher Perfero, to stand trial for her crime of absconsion.'

With a brief bow that was bordering on disrespectful toward the still-gaping king, the head wizard stalked from the room, followed closely by Mikel's wife and child. The enormous double doors magically closed behind them with a bang. The crowd of dragons erupted into excited conversation. The noise was deafening to Rachaya, causing her ears to ring, and she felt desperate to escape this now-oppressive chamber. Just as the room began to close in on her Mikel grabbed her by the elbow and led her from the room. Krishn and Mikel escorted her wordlessly back to her apartments. They barred the door behind them.

Mikel's eyes were still a furious green, but his skin had cooled down. He raked his fingers through his hair.

'I am so sorry, Princess. My own wife . . .' he said.

'What happens now?' asked Rachaya. She was beginning to feel better now that she was away from her second large crowd that day.

'That all depends on the contents of the court summons.' Mikel took the scroll from her numb fingers. He cursed. Krishn looked over his shoulder and scanned the document. He covered his face with his hands and groaned.

Rachaya fell into the nearest chair. 'Is it that bad?'

'They have set the court date for tomorrow morning, giving you no time to prepare a case,' Mikel said. 'I am going to kill Anjela.'

'No, that's good,' said Rachaya, her ears still ringing. 'That has to be a good thing.' Mikel and Krishn were looking at her with disbelief. 'No, really,' she said. 'The sooner this is over the sooner we can move on and build a life for ourselves here.'

Mikel knelt down before her. 'Rachaya, the king has done what he can for you by making you his heir, but he cannot do anything more. He has neither the strength nor the courage to naysay the wizards. If found guilty you will be punished by death. The wizards have more power here than you think. We can hide you, if you'd like? Adara managed to hide for a very long time.' He reached out and took her hand. 'I swear to you, I will find a way to keep you safe.'

Krishn sat down beside her and took her other hand. 'We will not serve you up like some fancy meal for these evil wizards.'

Tears welled in Rachaya's eyes. She wrenched her hands free to wipe the moisture away. 'I will face them,' she said. 'I will defeat them. I have to. I will not run and hide.' She looked at the prince. 'I am sorry, Mikel. I don't want to offend your people and I cannot even imagine how it happened, but the dragons are nothing but cowards when standing before the wizards. This has gone on too long – a day, a *minute*, is too long. My mother taught me that dragons are strong. They're *fierce*. Mikel, dragons are supposed to be fearless. I will show them all that I am a dragon who will not be crushed by the will of the wizards.'

Rachaya's voice gained strength as she talked, and she felt her fear dissipate. 'I will show the dragons that their future queen has come home and she will be a force to be reckoned with.' She smiled ruefully. 'Or I will be found guilty and I will die. Either way I will fight.'

CHAPTER 8

THE LAWFUL INFLICTION OF DEATH

Rachaya took a sip of tea. Her movements were mechanical, like that of the automatons the travelling minstrels brought to Cryll last year. She sat in a small antechamber, awaiting her dance with death. She felt . . . well actually, she didn't really feel anything at all. Sometime during the sleepless night she had lost all sense of feeling. A calm numbness had transcended in its stead.

Her name was called and she barely registered the sound. Her father hugged her one last time; she barely noticed that he was there. Placing one foot in front of the other, Rachaya approached her fate.

Seven bearded men sat in a row. Seven bearded men who would doom her to death. Without acknowledging their presence, Rachaya ascended the steps and took her seat upon the dais. Her coronet glistened among her red hair. The princess folded her hands in her lap and patiently waited for the proceedings to begin.

Mathonwy rose to his feet and the buzzing of whispered voices stopped in an instant.

'We, the Assembly's Council Representatives of Noble and Honourable Wizards, have gathered here today to bear witness to the trial of Crown Princess Rachaya Butcher Perfero for the breach of Statute Four-Six-One-Two. The trial will be overseen by myself, Head Wizard Mathonwy. Sitting with me in judgement today, as per Wizard Law, are Wizards Beli, Og, Math, Gideon, Arawn and Pell.' Mathonwy's bushy grey beard quivered, his black eyes glittering angrily. 'Crown Princess

Rachaya Butcher Perfero stands accused of the heinous crime of living within the bounds of the *human* world, utterly untrained, wielding her powers of dragon magic to control the humans.'

Rachaya's protectively numb bubble burst. She gaped at the head wizard with disbelief. Never in her life had she tried to control a human. She looked across at Mikel for support, but his face was very carefully blank of all emotion. Rachaya tried to do the same.

Head Wizard Mathonwy continued. 'I am sure I do not need to impress upon you, virtuous dragons, the dangers that such a severe breach of security could wreak upon Fyrebyrne Island and its inhabitants. As such, in the case of a guilty verdict, the Assembly's Council Representatives of Noble and Honourable Wizards will be seeking the maximum penalty – the lawful infliction of death.'

The watchful dragons gasped with horror. One water dragon fainted from the shock. His companion splashed water on his face by shooting it from her fingertips. Rachaya, however, did not react at all. She had been expecting this. It wasn't for her to worry about what the punishment was. Her only concern was to figure out how she could get out of this mess. She used the cover of the excited audience to examine the wizards more closely. Each of them was dressed in a flowing robe similar to Mathonwy's, but every robe was of a different colour. The wizards wore identical grim expressions on their bearded faces – all, that is, except for the much younger, raven-haired wizard at the far end of the row, the wizard Mathonwy had called Math. This wizard looked so much like Mathonwy, with the same pointed nose and thin lips, yet his eyes were a soft grey, rather than a glittering black. Within their depths Rachaya felt her first stirrings of hope. It was almost as if, although certainly not an ally, this wizard had not quite decided to be her enemy, either.

Head Wizard Mathonwy raised his hand for silence and the room fell quiet once more.

'The evidence,' he said, 'provided to me, Head Wizard Mathonwy of the First Order, by the Most-Honourable Lady Anjela Serena Perfero, is stated as thus: that the defendant was found in the human village of Cryll in the Kingdom of Rhyll, by the dragon prince, Mikel Aramus Perfero. That the defendant had, in a fit of rage and through her power of telekinesis, transported and rendered a boy, not yet six years old, entirely unconscious. The defendant then, no doubt to remove all evidence, set dragon fire upon the school, burning it completely to the ground.'

While the dragons in the audience gasped and shrieked, hot anger surged through Rachaya's body. How dare he spout such blatant lies! She struggled against the urge to jump up out of her seat.

'The Most-Royal Prince Mikel Aramus Perfero captured the defendant, bringing her here to Fyrebyrne Island where she can, thankfully, be brought to justice.' The head wizard turned from the crowd and faced the princess. 'Crown Princess Rachaya Butcher Perfero, did you, as stated, live within the bounds of the human world?'

'Yes, but—'

'And did you, as has been stated before the council, commit such heinous acts of magic within the *human* world?'

'No! I would—'

'Yes, you would. An admission!' roared Mathonwy.

Rachaya's hot anger turned to rage. She had been trying to say that she would never do such a thing. White-hot fire flew out from Rachaya's fingertips, scorching the arms of the chair she was gripping so tightly. The head wizard clapped his hands together in triumph.

'In the light of such damning evidence,' he declared, 'the Assembly's Council of Representatives of Noble and Honourable Wizards has no other choice than to find the defendant GUIL—'

'Head Wizard Mathonwy!' cut in the young wizard at the end of the table. 'If I may interrupt you for just a moment?'

Rachaya leant forward on her chair, gripping the smoking arm rests. A ripple of excitement spread around the room. No-one ever dared to interrupt the head wizard!

'It appears to me,' the young wizard continued, 'that we have yet to ascertain whether or not the young defendant has ever transformed into her dragon body.'

'That has no relevance to this case,' he replied. The look Head Wizard Mathonwy shot at Wizard Math would have withered a watermelon. The young wizard merely shrugged.

'It pains me to contradict you, Father, but I am very much afraid that it does,' replied the young wizard. 'Under Act three point six of the *Dragon Protection Mandate*, of the year seven-three-four, it clearly states that a dragon who has not yet made the transformation into their full dragon body is to be legally considered an infant. As such, no matter their age, such a dragon is to be deemed innocent of any crime in the eyes of the law.'

The young wizard bent down to straighten up some of his papers. 'I'm surprised you have forgotten, Father. You wrote that law to protect dragons from the crimes of their parents, should they remove their children from the island.'

Once his papers were nice and tidy, the Wizard Math straightened up to face Rachaya.

'Crown Princess Rachaya Butcher Perfero, have you ever made the full transformation into your dragon body?'

Rachaya shook her head adamantly. 'No,' she said. 'I have not.' She could have sworn she saw the ghost of a smile form on the young wizard's lips, but it was gone in an instant.

'Head Wizard Mathonwy, both the defendant and her father had declared the same to myself and the king,' said Mikel. There was no doubt about the smile on *his* face.

Head Wizard Mathonwy slammed his fist down on the table. 'Very well,' he said through gritted teeth. 'We declare the defendant to be an infant until such a time as she completes her first full transformation.' He shook his head. 'Therefore, the Assembly's Council Representatives of Noble and Honourable Wizards, on the authority of the Wizard Assembly, has no choice other than to declare the defendant not guilty.'

He shot Rachaya a look of pure hatred. 'But let me be clear, Crown Princess. You are treading a very fine line. You are to attend the Wyvold the Fierce School for Dragons as soon as it reopens for the new school year. Every misstep, any misbehaviour, will be noted and logged. I will *not* tolerate law-breakers on Fyrebyrne Island.'

'Yes, sir,' Rachaya said. Mathonwy held her gaze for a moment, and she was under no illusions. He had meant every word.

'Oh, and Wizard Math. My son,' he said to the young wizard at the end of the row. 'It warms my heart to see you developing such a fondness for dragons. It will set you in good stead, my child. I have been looking for a new wizard to fulfil the post of school chancellor. A most *rewarding* role, with hours of important meetings to attend and lunches with Wyvold's illustrious principal. I am convinced you are perfect for the role. Consider yourself hired.'

Mathonwy scooped up his papers. 'Court adjourned,' he snapped before stalking from the room. One by one the other wizards followed him, shaking their heads as they went.

Rachaya's life had been spared. She may have made a mortal enemy in the process, but for now her life had been saved by a legal loophole and a young wizard brave enough to speak up for her. Rachaya smiled her thanks to Wizard Math as Mikel dragged her from the room.

Her father was waiting for her in her apartments. She burst into tears the moment she saw him.

'Mikel!' he growled. 'You said it would be—'

'It's okay, Dad,' she said, running into his arms. 'I'm safe.'

Krishn let out a sigh of relief and held her tight. 'I'm so glad you're alright,' he said before kissing the top of her head.

Movement from the doorway caught Rachaya's eye. She looked up to see Mikel's son, Hektor, standing there with a scowl that mirrored his mother's.

'So you'll be joining me at Wyvolds, I suppose,' he said. 'I'd like to know how you intend to pass when you have a *human* for a father.'

'Hektor, that's enough!' Mikel said. The boy had already turned and fled, but not without first giving Rachaya something entirely new to worry about. Would her human blood make her fail at being a dragon?

CHAPTER 9

A CORONATION CARNIVAL

'You're throwing her a what?'

Rachaya jerked her hand back from the door handle at the sound of Lady Anjela's acid tones coming from inside the room. Rachaya was well and truly lost, then – she had thought she was opening the door to her own rooms. Sure, she knew it was wrong to eavesdrop, but she leant in closer to the door anyway.

'I don't know why you're so outraged,' Mikel was saying. 'Each prince or princess is thrown a celebratory party following their coronation as heir apparent. Even I had one following my investiture as heir presumptive.'

'But she *stole* the crown from you. Why should you be the one to throw her a blasted party?'

The young princess could hear pottery shatter against the wall. The room grew hot – so hot that Rachaya could feel the heat seeping through the door. It was at odds with how cold Mikel's voice was when he spoke next.

'Do that again and it may very well be the last thing you do within this castle,' he said.

'You dare to threaten me?'

Rachaya leant in closer to the door despite the heat.

'Threaten? No, not exactly. But I will offer you an ultimatum. Either you graciously accept the new princess and make her feel welcome, or you pack your bags and leave Perfero Castle for good.'

'You would do that?' Lady Anjela's voice had reached a high pitch now. 'What of our son?'

'Hektor is not involved with this, nor would I have you make him so. This family must stand shoulder to shoulder in solidarity, now more so than ever.' He paused. 'I will know your answer by your presence or absence at Rachaya's Coronation Carnival.'

Rachaya stifled a scream when a hand squeezed her arm. She whipped around and came face-to-face with a very old woman with pure white hair.

'Come with me, my dear,' said the lady, leading Rachaya away from the door and the argument within.

'A young lady should never listen at keyholes, child,' said the woman. 'That's what servants are for. They're always more than happy to pass on any gossip.'

'Who are you?' asked Rachaya.

'True, we haven't met, but I've heard so much about you I feel I know you already.' She threw open a nearby door, revealing a comfortable sitting room. 'Sit down. I'll order us some tea,' the old woman said.

'But who *are* you?' Rachaya insisted.

'Lady Persefone. Mikel's mother.'

Rachaya instinctively relaxed. The woman even had Mikel's easy smile and kind face.

'I didn't mean to listen in – I got lost – I thought I was at my rooms,' she said.

'And yet you lingered.' The corner of the lady's mouth twitched. 'Oh, I'm not angry, Princess,' she said. 'I'm grateful to you. I was getting bored up here on my own. Mikel's been too busy to visit of late.'

Rachaya felt guilty. That was her fault, too. Lady Persefone sat down beside her and placed a hand on her knee.

'I can see you are blaming yourself. That needs to stop right away. None of this is your fault. Now, have a biscuit.'

Rachaya took a biscuit and bit into it, but she spat it out right away.

'That's not a biscuit!' she cried. 'It's made of meat!'

'How else do you expect them to be made, girl? Now look what you've done – such a waste of good meat.'

Rachaya wiped her mouth with the back of her hand. 'Back home biscuits are made from flour and butter, things like that.'

'Ha! Grains? I prefer to leave those for the air dragons. Go on, have another try. They're delicious.'

Rachaya took another bite, more prepared this time. The meat had been seasoned lightly, and the old lady was right. It was quite tasty.

'So you're not mad at me for taking Mikel's crown?'

'Of course not! He'd never have time for his poor old mum if he were king. And as to that wife of his, I hate to say it, but boy does she ever have a stick up her buttocks. This may well go a long way toward removing it.'

Rachaya snorted out her biscuit.

'Oh, come on, don't tell me you hadn't noticed,' Lady Persefone said with great innocence.

Tea was brought in and Rachaya was really beginning to enjoy herself when Mikel and Krishn burst into the room, both looking frantic.

'There you are! We've been looking all over for you,' Mikel said.

Krishn was a lot calmer than the prince. 'I knew you'd just be lost,' he said. 'I'm only glad you were able to have a cup of tea while you were at it.'

'Now there's a sensible man,' said Lady Persefone. 'Come, join us.'

Both men sat down, but Mikel still seemed agitated. He kept jiggling his leg up and down, shaking the tea tray so it rattled.

'Oh, for goodness sake, Mikel, tell us what's troubling you,' said Lady Persefone. 'You only ever fidget when you have something on your mind.'

Mikel forced out a smile. 'Nothing's bothering me, Mother,' he said. 'But I do have a big task ahead of me – preparing the princess' Coronation Carnival.'

The old lady clapped her hands together with delight. 'Oh, Mikel, that will be wonderful! It's been an age since we've had a decent festival.'

'What's a Coronation Carnival?' asked Rachaya. She wasn't sure she was going to like the idea half as much as Lady Persefone seemed to.

'It's a celebration down in Perfero Village for your coronation as Crown Princess,' said Mikel. 'There'll be food, dancing, music – it'll be great fun.'

'And it will coincide with your birthday,' said Krishn. 'I was worried we wouldn't be able to celebrate properly this year since so much has happened lately.'

'I won't have to make a speech or anything, will I?'

'Just a teensy, tiny, little one,' said Mikel. 'What do you say?'

Rachaya smiled weakly. 'I don't really have a choice, do I?'

Mikel grinned broadly, his smile genuine this time. 'Nope,' he said.

***

Rachaya stood in front of the mirror in her new silk dress which was embedded with jewels. A small golden crown nestled within her red hair.

'What am I going to say?' she asked. She felt more nervous than she had at the Wizard trial. Death seemed an easier option than giving a speech to an entire village.

'Just thank everyone for coming along and welcoming you to the island,' her father said. He gripped her shoulder. 'You'll be fine. They'll love you.'

'Not everyone does,' whispered Rachaya. 'Mikel's wife is really angry. She broke a pot.'

Krishn sighed. 'I'm not going to ask how you know that,' he said. 'But don't let her get you down. She may try her best to discomfort you, but she will only succeed if you let her.'

With one last squeeze of her shoulder Krishn led the princess into the sitting room. Mikel and his mother were waiting to escort them down to the village. Lady Anjela was nowhere to be seen, although Lady Persefone's excitement easily made up for the absence of the other woman.

Small orbs of warm orange fire floated quietly in the calm night sky, lighting their path through the castle grounds and down to the local village. The sound of merry music and laughter reached their ears. Rachaya gripped her father's arm tightly as they rounded a corner and she caught her first sight of Perfero Village and its occupants. Her breath caught in her throat. The villagers had erected a stage that looked uncannily like the platform that had been built for her in Cryll. But the demeanour of the dragons was different. They were smiling and laughing, sharing food and dancing. Earth, air, fire and water: all the different dragons were there, ready to celebrate Rachaya's coronation.

Mikel led them through the crowd, introducing Rachaya to dragons as they passed. The prince seemed to know everybody, and everyone was in a good mood. They greeted Rachaya with a friendly manner laced with polite curiosity. The butcher, Lance Groundig, was especially pleased to meet her.

'I heard you have the word 'butcher' in your name,' he said, clasping her small hand in his big beefy one. 'Is that because you favour the profession? Many dragons do.'

'My father's a butcher,' she explained. The butcher immediately forgot her, dropping her hand and rushing forward to take Krishn's instead. The two butchers spent many happy minutes exchanging butchery techniques. They were interrupted by an ancient air dragon.

'Grandpa Breeze, everyone calls me,' he said. 'I live up in the Eyrie, of course, but came down just to meet you.' He pressed a candy bar into her hand. 'Just a little gift from my confectionary shop.' He smiled and hurried off.

Rachaya met all kinds of dragons, every one of them pleased to meet her. They were even welcoming of her father once they found out he was an accomplished butcher. It turned out that all of them, with the exception of air dragons, loved meat.

They walked past stalls of food with hand-painted signs above them.

'Curry so hot it will make you breathe fire,' Rachaya read. Next to it was a candy stand. 'Insect pops – every fifth pop has a surprise scorpion tail in it!' Rachaya decided then and there that she wouldn't eat the candy bar Grandpa Breeze had given to her.

Although she could easily read the bottom half of all the signs, Rachaya could not make out the strange symbols on the top halves. She had never seen writing like it before.

'They're written in Dragon Tongue,' Mikel explained. 'You will learn the runes when you go to Wyvolds.'

They approached the stage and Rachaya's nerves returned with full force.

'You'll be fine,' whispered Krishn before merging with the rest of the crowd. Lady Persefone linked arms with her and Rachaya was grateful for the support. They ascended the stairs behind Mikel. Lady Anjela may have been vindictive but she wasn't stupid. To Rachaya's surprise, the lady was already up on the stage, standing beside the king. She had a pained smile painted upon her face. Hektor stood a little behind his mother, taking no such trouble to hide his displeasure at being there. Lady Anjela curtseyed to the new princess, earning a nod of approval from her husband. Mikel took his place beside his wife. Lady Persefone patted Rachaya's hand before moving toward the back of the family, leaving Rachaya alone at the front and centre of the stage. The entire village waited patiently for her to speak. Rachaya opened her mouth to begin her speech, but was halted by the arrival of a very old earth dragon, whose wrinkled skin hung loosely over bulging muscles. He held before him a purple velvet cushion, atop of which sat a pile of glittering jewels in a rainbow of colour.

'On behalf of the earth dragons I, Elder Duggett, welcome Crown Princess Rachaya to Perfero Village,' he said. The crowd burst into applause as Rachaya accepted the gift and thanked the dragon. He was followed by an air dragon so old he made Grandpa Breeze seem youthful. He presented the princess with a beautiful fountain pen and her very own wax seal. An elderly water dragon came after him, so fat she needed a cane to walk, and presented Rachaya with a string of pearls. The final dragon, an elderly fire dragon, presented her with a beautiful ceremonial sword. After much bowing and curtseying the elders left her alone on the stage once more. Now, it appeared, was the time to make her dreaded speech. With nothing else for it, she began to speak.

Rachaya's first words came out as a squeak. She desperately looked through the crowd for her father. She found him next to the butcher, Lance Goundig. Krishn gave her a reassuring smile and her voice grew stronger. She scurried from the stage the moment she had finished speaking, in desperate need of some quiet so she could clear her head. Her blood was pounding in her head and her hands were shaking – facing the wizards had been easier.

Rachaya somehow managed to find a quiet place behind an empty kebab stand. 'No salad will be found in *our* kebabs,' she read on the sign above it. The princess sank down onto the ground, pulled her knees up to her chest, and began to slowly count to ten. Interrupted by the shuffling of feet nearby, she looked up to find a dark-haired boy of around her own age reaching into the kebab stand. He snatched his hand back and flushed a deep scarlet when he realised that the princess was watching him. His clothing was ragged and patched, his hair greasy and unkempt. Rachaya felt guilty, sitting there in her finery staring at this destitute boy. She lowered her eyes and the boy scampered.

'Ah, so you've met Morhol, poor lad,' said Mikel, appearing out of the shadows. 'He'll be starting Wyvolds this year, too, I believe.' He sat down on the ground beside Rachaya. 'Once you're at school you can be normal again – everyone will forget you are the princess and you'll be treated the same as all the other students. Your mother and I loved Wyvolds for that very reason.'

'I don't really mind it so much,' said Rachaya. 'Everyone's been so kind to me. I just don't like making speeches.'

Mikel laughed. 'I've never much cared for them myself,' he said. 'And of course everyone's nice. They loved your mother. No-one was pleased when I took Adara's place, although they got used to the notion over time. We're all just happy that the rightful succession has been restored. You simply have to keep everyone on your side and you'll have a long and peaceful reign.'

Mikel helped Rachaya to her feet and led her back into the crowd. She kept her eye out for the ragged boy, Morhol, but she didn't see him again.

CHAPTER 10

PREPARING FOR WYVOLDS

Lady Anjela narrowed her eyes. 'No, make the blazer bigger. She'll grow out of that one within six months.'

Rachaya looked up pleadingly at Krishn but he shook his head. At Mikel's suggestion Lady Anjela had agreed to help ready Rachaya for school, since Krishn had no idea what dragons would need for their education, and there was no way he was going to interfere when she was being so helpful.

'I'll look ridiculous in a bigger blazer,' she said.

'Nonsense,' said Lady Anjela, 'you'll look just like everybody else.' The lady furrowed her brow. 'I agree that the jodhpurs need to be skin-tight, though. We can't have them getting caught in your scales when you transform.'

She sent the tiny air dragon, Jecca Waft, off to fetch some better sizes.

'Why do we have to do all this here? I was hoping to see the village again,' said Rachaya.

Lady Anjela reached out and straightened the princess' tie. 'A princess never simply goes shopping. Shopping comes to her.'

Rachaya was beginning to recognise these maxims of Lady Anjela's. Already she hated them.

Jecca returned with a larger blazer and smaller jodhpurs, and Rachaya went behind the screen to try them on. They had agreed on giving her that much privacy, at least. She came back out to show the adults the new sizes. She felt ridiculous – the sleeves draped down over her hands and the blazer almost reached her knees.

'Perfect!' said Lady Anjela, clapping her hands.

'Dad, please, it's way too big.'

'Sorry, Chia, I agree with Lady Anjela's judgement on this. You'll grow into it in no time.'

Rachaya was slightly mollified when the stationer arrived. She got a lovely set of leather-bound notebooks, and Lady Anjela even let her pick the fancy pencils over the plain ones.

'They'll last much longer,' noted the lady.

Rachaya was the most excited by the arrival of the armourer, Bert Oldmine, a burly earth dragon who caused Lady Anjela to scowl and Rachaya to smile.

'So, you're the young princess, eh?' He rubbed his hands together. 'Well, there's not much to yeh, but we'll see about some nice bows for yeh. Always a good place to start for a lass.' He handed Rachaya a simple bow and showed her how to hold it. 'Now, you'll struggle at first to pull back the string, o'course, but give it a try anyway.'

Rachaya held her fingers carefully, just as the armourer had shown her, and pulled back the string with ease. The armourer's jaw dropped. Krishn grinned proudly at his daughter.

'Well, I'll be. Maybe you'll be a warrior princess after all. You're certainly stronger than I gave you credit for.'

'She gets that from working in the butcher's shop with me,' said Krishn.

Oldmine nodded his approval. 'Is that so? I don't hold with this nonsense of namby-pambying young girls. Teach 'em to be brave and strong an' they will be.' He cocked an eyebrow at Krishn. 'I reckon she'll be able to handle a full battleaxe.'

'Absolutely not,' said Lady Anjela. 'School supplies only. A beginner's sword, bow and quiver, and a small dagger. The rest can wait until she's older.'

The armourer looked disappointed, although not as disappointed as Rachaya.

'As you wish, m'lady,' he said with a small bow.

The next vendor to arrive was Petal Harvest, from Harvest Herbery. The old water dragon smelled strongly of leaf litter and had a smudge of dirt on her nose. Lady Anjela's scowl somehow increased, and she had the cheery herbalist in and out of the castle in record time.

Lady Anjela haggled with the bookseller over the cost of Rachaya's text books and had a rune dictionary thrown in for free. She was very pleased with herself – more pleased than Rachaya had ever seen her – until Mikel walked into the room. Trotting in behind him, with a loop of rope tied around its long feathered neck, was a large wingless bird with green plumage. It honked at them in greeting.

'You bought her an *oka*?' asked Lady Anjela.

'Krishn chipped in, too,' Mikel replied cheerfully. 'For her birthday.'

'*But why is it in the castle*?' Lady Anjela cried in a high-pitched voice. 'Look at the rug!'

Rachaya, Krishn and Mikel bit back their laughter. Thick white blobs now decorated the otherwise pristine carpet. The oka honked again, very pleased with the attention it was getting.

'GET IT OUT OF HERE!'

'Come on, Rachaya, I'll show you where the oka stables are.'

The trio left Lady Anjela calling for a servant to 'clean the rug for pity's sake!'

As they walked down to the stables the oka kept trying to pat itself on Rachaya's hand.

'She likes you,' said Mikel. 'What'll you call her?'

She scratched the bird's bony head thoughtfully. 'Nyssa,' she said.

Tibbles caught up with them in the castle grounds, but didn't seem to like Nyssa nearly as much as Nyssa liked her. The oka tried to rub its head against the cat's fur. Tibbles swatted at the bird before running off.

'I think Tibbles might be jealous,' Rachaya said.

'Yes, but you can't ride Tibbles,' said Mikel.

'Ride her?'

'Dragons trained okas to be ridden like horses,' Krishn explained. 'Unlike horses, okas are too stupid to be afraid of the smell of dragons.'

'They fear no predators,' said Mikel. Nyssa honked in agreement.

Mikel had already organised a stall for Nyssa in among the other palace okas. They were all different colours, from pinks and purples to oranges and browns, and they were all incredibly dimwitted. They instantly became Rachaya's favourite type of animal.

Nyssa sighed loudly when she realised they were going to leave without her. Rachaya gave the bird a final pat, sorry to be leaving her behind.

That night the family threw her a surprise dinner party in honour of her birthday. The king gave Rachaya a delicate gold necklace and Lady Persefone gave her a grooming kit for her oka. Even Lady Anjela had instructed a servant to bake her a cake. Everyone did their best to make Rachaya feel special; everyone except Hektor. He refused to go to the dinner, and had vowed to never speak to the 'usurper' princess.

'At least he acknowledges that I'm a princess,' Rachaya said dryly.

'Try to cut him some slack, Chia,' her father said afterward. 'Hektor was born believing he would one day be king. He's had his whole world pulled out from under him. The poor kid's going to need some time to adjust.'

Rachaya was prepared to give Hektor some time, until later that night when the young lord beat her up.

Rachaya had gone down to the stables to say goodnight to Nyssa. As she headed back up to the castle she was grabbed from behind by the young lord and pressed up against a rough stone wall. She struggled against his grasp, but he was much bigger than her.

'My father wants me to keep an eye on you at school. He wants us to be *friends*. But it's not going to happen, do you hear?'

Hektor's breath felt hot and unpleasant against her ear. She nodded, but he wasn't finished with her yet.

'You will never speak to me, nor any of my friends. You are not to speak about me to anyone. If you do, I will know. Oh, and mention this little "chat" to anyone and I will destroy you.'

Hektor pushed Rachaya roughly before releasing her. She dropped to the ground and watched him saunter away as if he didn't have a care in the world. She glared at his retreating figure and felt hot anger bubble up in her stomach, much as it had during the Wizard trial. How dare he threaten her! Did he really think she wanted such a pompous ass for a friend?

The princess launched to her feet and patted down her dress. She would show him. She would go about her business as if he didn't even exist. She would prove to everyone that she would make a far better queen than he ever would a king. She was almost grateful to the young lord. Rachaya had been beginning to let her guard down around Lady Anjela, but here was a reminder that not everyone was as pleased about her existence as Mikel and Lady Persefone were.

Cut Hektor some slack? Rachaya didn't think so.

CHAPTER 11

THE TURTLE PRINCIPAL

Rachaya pulled on her much-too-big blazer and wrinkled her nose at her reflection in the mirror. She looked far from being a princess now. How had she transformed so quickly into just another school kid? She looked pale and scared, which perfectly matched her roiling stomach filled with butterflies. With one last grimace at her reflection, Rachaya began to drag her suitcase down to the castle lawn.

Mikel laughed when he saw her. 'What on Escoria are you carrying your suitcase for? Here, allow me.' He snapped his fingers and her suitcase disappeared.

'What did you do? Where has it gone?' Rachaya cried. If he had destroyed her suitcase . . . she'd spent hours packing it!

'Relax, Chia, he's just cached it,' said her father, since Mikel was laughing too hard at Rachaya's reaction to reply. 'Your mother used to do it all the time just to annoy me.'

'Cached it?'

'Sure,' said Mikel, gulping down his laughter. 'I've stored it in a secret place of mine, to be retrieved later, at my convenience.' He gave a little bow. 'You're welcome.'

'When do I learn how to do that?'

'You won't learn magic like that at Wyvolds, I'm afraid. It's a little trick Adara taught me. Us Perferos have always had stronger magic than other dragons. It's how we ended up being the ruling monarchs.'

'So you can teach me?'

'Only if your father allows it.'

She turned to her father hopefully.

'He can hardly teach you right now, Chia. We have to get you to school,' her father said. 'You'll have more than enough to learn in the coming weeks. Maybe once you're home for the holidays.'

Rachaya's smile faded. She had forgotten she wouldn't see her father again for weeks and weeks. She ran into his arms.

'I'll miss you,' she said.

'No you won't, you'll be too busy doing dragony things,' he replied, but he held her tightly.

'Write to me?'

'Just you try to stop me.'

Rachaya wiped away her tears, hoping Mikel hadn't noticed them, but he was far from laughing at her. He clapped her on the back kindly.

'I'll look after your dad, kiddo,' he said. 'Don't forget you can contact us anytime you need anything – anything at all. Now, come on. You don't want to be late on your first day.'

The prince transformed into his yellow dragon body. Rachaya paid close attention this time. Hopefully she would soon be transforming herself. She climbed up his rough, scaly shoulder and sat down at the base of his neck. Tibbles leapt up and took a seat beside her. When no-one complained, Rachaya smiled a true smile for the first time that morning. Even if everyone hated her she would have at least one friend at school. She looked down at her father and waved one last goodbye to him. Krishn looked back up at her wistfully, his jaw clenched. Suddenly he grinned and waved back at her.

'I'm so proud of you,' he called. 'Your mother would be, too.'

Mikel launched himself into the air and Rachaya had to grip on to his scales tightly. Her father, and everything that represented humanity, receded until it was no more than a speck on the landscape.

Mikel soared through the air, carrying Rachaya toward her future. From now on she was a bona fide dragon. The thought sent thrills up her spine. She was going to be a dragon.

No.

She was already a dragon.

The princess held on to that thought as the landscape flashed by her and the unknown drew nearer and nearer.

Rivers, lakes, forests, farmlands, plains, wastelands – a myriad of landscapes flashed by in an astonishingly short space of time. This truly was a strange island. Rachaya's eyes were stinging from the wind and eventually she had to close them. She didn't reopen them again until Tibbles began clawing at her arm. She opened her eyes to catch her first sight of her new school – the Wyvold the Fierce School for Dragons.

Rachaya's school in Cryll had been a tiny tin shed in the centre of the village. Wyvolds was enormous by comparison. A multitude of buildings – some large, some small – were spread out around a large grassy oval. Each building was painted a different, vibrant colour, and embossed on each roof was the school crest.

Rachaya was not the only student to be arriving by air. Large, stately fire dragons dotted the sky, carrying their progeny on their backs in a graceful tapestry of reds, oranges, yellows, purples and blacks. Diminutive air dragons soared through the sky, too. They zipped around their much larger counterparts, carrying their children in their spindly arms. Their colouration was much more pale, a collection of light blues, greys, silvers and yellows. They made their acrobatics look easy, and Rachaya couldn't help but feel slightly envious of their superior flying.

There was a large lake at the far end of the school's grounds. From beneath the rippling surface blubbery water dragons emerged, their clinging children enshrouded in translucent air bubbles. Their hides glistened in shades of browns, greens, greys and blues.

On the opposite side of the lawn burly earth dragons emerged, seemingly from out of nowhere. Mikel descended a little, and Rachaya could see that they were coming from out of a cavernous hole in the ground.

The earth dragons were by far the most gruesome, terrifying dragons of the lot. They were just so big, in every possible sense of the word, with muscular flanks and two dangerous-looking horns perched atop their heads. The students clinging to their backs were covered in a variety of dirt, matching the colour of the dragons themselves – browns, blacks, greys, reds; there was even an earth dragon the colour of sand.

The student body was small. There were only about a hundred students in total enrolled at Wyvolds. But with the enormous adult dragons dropping their children off, there seemed to be far more people gathered on the landing lawn than there actually was. Rachaya held Mikel's scales as tightly as her nerves gripped her.

Mikel held his sail-like wings out to his sides and slowly drifted down to the ground. Remembering how last time he had thrown them from his back, Rachaya wasted no time in scrambling down his shoulder. He began transforming the moment her feet touched the grass. Tibbles had already scampered away to goodness knew where by the time Mikel was in his human form again.

Dragons greeted dragons with excitement and hugs. Rachaya knew nobody except Hektor, who had landed on the other side of the oval atop his mother's dull orange back, so she stood there stupidly, pushing back the cuffs of her over-long blazer. At least she couldn't feel any worse than this.

Mikel draped an arm around her shoulder.

'Ready to face the principal?' he asked cheerfully.

She had been wrong. She could feel worse. A lot worse.

'Why do I need to see the principal?' she squeaked.

'Relax, Rachaya. All Level 1 students meet with Principal Thestral before enrolling at Wyvolds. Your interview's just a bit later than everyone else's since you weren't on Fyrebyrne Island at the end of last year.'

He started to walk off, dragging her along with him. They entered a tall building with heavy oak doors. Inside was an airy office with hard chairs for visitors pushed to one side. The centre of the floor was inlaid with the school crest, as was the furthermost wall. Beneath this wall sat a cluttered reception desk. A middle-aged, wiry woman wearing wing-tipped glasses perched behind the desk. Her angry expression reminded Rachaya so much of Lady Anjela that she looked to the other two, equally messy desks instead. A plump, cheerful-looking woman with buckteeth manned one desk, but she was already talking to another parent. The other desk was occupied by a tiny woman whose white hair fluttered about her face in wisps. She looked like she was a very kind woman, but at this moment she was fast asleep, snoring gently into her paperwork. With a shrug of his shoulders Mikel approached the angry, wing-tipped gorgon, whose nostrils flared wider the closer he got.

'I'm here to see Principal Thestral,' he said with much more confidence than Rachaya would have had.

'NAME,' she barked.

'Mikel Perfero, escorting Rachaya Butcher Perfero.'

The woman's lips thinned and her eyes squinted with distrust behind her bejewelled spectacles. With a sniff she rose from her seat and stormed across the room, exiting via a side door. Mikel grinned down at Rachaya and gave her a conspiratorial wink.

'That was Mrs Vulcan,' he whispered. 'She was just as, er . . . *friendly* when I was a student here. It's best to stay on her good side.'

'She has a good side?' Rachaya asked.

Mrs Vulcan didn't leave them waiting for long. She returned to her desk and sat back down, acting for all the world as if Rachaya and Mikel were not still standing there. Thankfully, she was soon followed by the principal, Mr Thestral. He came shuffling into the room and ushered for them to follow him into his office.

The principal was a diminutive man who strongly resembled a turtle. He had a shiny, bald head, inch-thick glasses that he constantly pushed back up onto the bridge of his nose and, despite being stick-thin elsewhere, had a large, round belly that protruded from his waist like a bowling ball. He was not exactly a man to inspire awe among the student body.

Mr Thestral sat down behind a desk that was much too big for him and stared unblinkingly up at Rachaya through magnified eyes. The princess tried to hold his gaze until her eyes started to water. After several silent minutes, Mikel cleared his throat. The principal jumped right up out of his seat, landing back down with a *whump*. Rachaya blinked furiously when the principal finally broke eye contact to look down at the ledger in front of him.

'Yes, now, let me see,' he said. 'Name: Rachaya Butcher Perfero.' He chuckled. 'There's certainly no mistaking the Perfero red hair . . . Now, what's the princess' age?' he asked Mikel. He spoke in a nasally, tremulous voice that made him sound as if he had a permanent head cold.

'Just turned thirteen.'

'Has she transformed?'

'No.'

'Performed fire magic?'

'Briefly.'

'Ah,' said the principal, his huge eyes back on Rachaya. 'Any hobbies, musical talents or sporting prowess that might benefit the school in any way?'

Rachaya's eyes watered under his unblinking gaze. 'No, sir.'

'Well, never mind, never mind.'

It took Rachaya a moment to realise that Mr Thestral had risen out of his seat. He was so tiny that there had been very little height change.

'All seems to be in order, then, Prince Mikel,' he said. 'I'll just arrange for an older student to come and show the princess to her dormitory.'

'Which dorm is she in?' asked Mikel. 'I need to send up her bags.'

Mr Thestral frowned; he no longer looked like a friendly turtle.

'May I remind you, Prince Mikel, that non-dragon magic is not permitted to be performed on school grounds. The young princess will do well to remember that, too, if she's at all like every other Perfero who has graced this school.'

Mikel shot the principal a winning smile.

'Why, Mr Thestral, I merely meant I would have a servant carry the princess' bags across for her. I would *never* break a Wyvold's rule.'

'Hmph. In that case you've changed considerably since your school days. She'll be in Dormitory 3.'

The principal shambled from the room in search of a student to guide Rachaya. The door clicked shut behind him.

'See, that wasn't so bad,' said Mikel. 'He's a bit eccentric, I admit, but he does a good job of running the school. He's an excellent administrator. He doesn't spend much time amongst the students, so you'll only ever see him when you get into trouble.' He winked at Rachaya. 'Just try not to make it too often. I'd like to keep my visits to the principal to a minimum.'

Mikel reached into his pocket and pulled out a bag that jangled merrily. He handed it to Rachaya. She looked at him blankly.

'Some treasure,' he said. 'In case you need to trade for anything.'

'Treasure?' The bag suddenly felt heavy in her hand. What if she lost it?

'All dragons carry treasure. We exchange it for goods and services. Like if you want to send a letter to your father, you give the airmailman some treasure and he'll send your letter across with the next stiff breeze.'

'Oh,' said Rachaya, 'you mean money.'

Mikel snorted. 'Worthless pieces of metal that humans pass from hand to hand? I don't think so. Dragons would never fall for such a stupid system. No, we use treasure from our family hoards. No-one gets ripped off that way.'

'Thank you.' Rachaya pocketed the treasure, making a mental note to store it somewhere safe as soon as she could.

The principal returned with a plump, curly-haired girl who was quite clearly a water dragon.

'I did one better than an older student,' he said. 'I found one of your dorm mates to help you. Princess, meet Lily Fisher.'

The girl curtseyed, causing Rachaya to blush with embarrassment.

'Just call me Rachaya,' she said.

'Well, off you girls go. I've got a mountain of paperwork to get through now that term has started.'

With a quick wave goodbye Mikel was gone, and Rachaya was propelled away from the only face familiar to her in the entire school.

CHAPTER 12

NEW FRIENDS

Lily Fisher spoke with the rapidity of a rushing river and Rachaya found it impossible to get a word in, which was lucky because she was completely tongue-tied. Lily led her across to the multicoloured dormitory building.

'Girls to the left, boys to the right,' explained Lily as they entered the building. 'You're in a dorm with me and four other girls. All up there's two fires, two waters, an air and an earth. The earth keeps crying – can't remember her name. I think she's upset because her earth friend was moved to another dorm to make room for you, but I think she should be pleased. After all, we have a *princess* in with us.'

Lily stopped triumphantly in the doorway to their dorm, oblivious to Rachaya's embarrassment. 'I've brought the *princess*,' she announced to the other girls. Lily skipped over to the other water dragon and began whispering excitedly with her. Bright red, embarrassed and alone, Rachaya located her bed at the far end of the room. She walked over to it, feeling as if every pair of eyes was on her, hoping she came across more confident than she felt. She knew this was her bed because Tibbles was already fast asleep on the bare mattress. She lifted the snoring cat off the bed and started to make it with the sheets that were neatly stacked on the bedside table.

Each bed had a small desk opposite it, a small chest of drawers and a cupboard. Rachaya busied herself with unpacking the suitcase Mikel had magically sent up to her room despite the principal's warnings. As she set up her area she built up the courage to talk to the other girls. Just as she was about to introduce herself a loud bell sounded. The other dragons filed out of the room and Rachaya followed them awkwardly, frustrated with herself for not speaking sooner. The group led her to a large hall where the entire school had assembled. Rachaya took a seat behind her dorm group and looked around her. She was beginning to be able to tell the difference between the dragon types. Air, small and wispy; earth, tall and brawny; fire, medium and lithe; water, chubby and cheerful. It was not just the students, but the teachers that seemed to fit the pattern, too. Dotted around the room, each teacher was supervising a small area of students. Rachaya distracted herself by trying to guess which of them would be teaching her classes.

Principal Thestral ambled onto the stage at the front of the hall and the teachers began to hush the students. The excited babble quietened and soon there was silence. A tiny boy with enormous grey eyes sat beside Rachaya, excitement shining from his face. He sat on the edge of his seat as the principal began to speak.

'I hope we're all ready for another great year at Wyvolds,' he said with a magically enhanced, but no-less nasally voice.

'Oh,' gasped the boy. 'Air magic. I hope I get to learn how to do that.' A nearby teacher hushed the boy and Rachaya smiled apologetically.

'For those of us who are new here, I will detail the way today will work,' Mr Thestral continued.

The boy next to Rachaya let out a squeak of excitement.

'Following this assembly we will each break off into Grade Level meetings, where timetables and homework diaries will be distributed.'

'Ooh,' said the boy.

'After dinner, recreational time has been allotted so that you can each set yourselves up for tomorrow. Lessons will begin at nine o'clock sharp.'

The boy next to Rachaya was so excited by the prospect of lessons starting he fell out of his seat. She bent over and helped him up.

'And now all that remains is for me to impress upon you all the responsibility that each and every one of you has to this school, to uphold the high standards of this institution.'

The boy next to Rachaya set his hand in a salute to the principal. He was beginning to attract the attention of the other students. A girl in front of Rachaya turned around and snorted at the sight of the boy's raised arm. She winked at Rachaya before turning back around.

Mr Thestral blinked down at the students through his thick glasses, a happy look on his face as if congratulating himself on a speech well made. He clapped his hands together and rubbed them.

'Well, then, what are you all waiting for? Off you go.'

As one, the students scrambled to their feet in a cacophony of sound.

'Can you believe we get *diaries*? And *timetables*!' the small boy said. 'I'm Reijko, by the way. Thanks for helping me up before.'

'I'm Rachaya, and that's okay,' she replied, but he was already off in pursuit of his new stationery. Rachaya looked wildly about her for a familiar face and thankfully caught sight of Lily in the swarm of students. She hurried forward to follow her out of the hall. Threading her way through the crowd, Rachaya caught up with the water dragon out on the landing lawn. Lily was standing with the other water dragon from their dorm, poring over a map of the school. The other students surged off in all directions, and very soon they were the only three students still standing there.

'Oh, Lissa, look! The Weaponry Dome is leagues away! Why do we have to go so far? We're never going to make it in time.' She pointed to a round building on the map.

'It's alright, look!' her cheerful friend said. 'It's just on the other side of the lawn. See that yellow building?'

Lily cheered up in an instant. 'That's nowhere near as far as it looks on the map,' she said. 'You coming?' she called to Rachaya as the two water dragons hurried off in the direction of the Weaponry Dome. Rachaya could see the last of the other Level 1 students disappear through the building's tall archway.

The trio followed the trill of students' voices into a large gladiators' pit. There they joined the other students, who were seated on the soft red sand. At their arrival the teacher began to count the students, his muscles rippling beneath his shirt as he pointed to each of the young dragons.

'He has to be an earth dragon for sure,' Rachaya whispered to Lily.

'Yes. Mr Ruffhead. He's the Level 1 coordinator.'

'We seem to be missing somebody,' Mr Ruffhead said when he had finished counting. At that moment Rachaya saw Morhol, the boy she had caught stealing food at her Coronation Carnival, slink in through the door. The teacher spotted him, too.

'Lost, were we?' asked Mr Ruffhead. 'Not to worry. I'm not going to bite your head off on the first day.'

He began to read out the roll, taking careful note of each student's face as they raised their hand and said 'here'.

'As your level coordinator, I am your first port of call should you need anything. I am also your teachers' first port of call should they catch you breaking school rules. Your school diary outlines these rules. Please take the time to familiarise yourself with them.'

Reijko immediately inched forward in his seat, his hands shaking as if he couldn't wait to get his hands on his crisp new diary. Rachaya could have sworn Mr Ruffhead was trying not to laugh at the small air dragon's reaction.

'Your diary also comes with a map in case you get lost. But don't forget, there are plenty of older students around to point you in the right direction. I recognise some of you from last year, too. If you have been at Wyvolds before, I expect you to help our new students out as much as you can. Students who are repeating Level 1, please raise your hands.' Several hands shot up around the room. 'The rest of you, these people can help you settle in to Wyvolds.'

Mr Ruffhead then went around the room handing out timetables and homework diaries. Reijko snatched his excitedly and immediately wrote his name in big letters across the front of it, beaming from ear to ear as he did so. Rachaya read through the list of subjects once she had received hers. They were the strangest list of topics she had ever seen and they were nothing like the classes she had studied at her village school. Dragon Studies and Fire Studies, Magical Education, Transformation, Gemology and Herbalism. And what, in all The Known Lands of Escoria, were Hopology and Personal Development?

Reijko's enthusiasm must have been infectious. Rachaya was beginning to feel very excited now that she could see her subjects in print. The bell sounded and Mr Ruffhead dismissed them all. Lily seemed to have forgotten about her again, so Rachaya trudged back across the lawn by herself, following the other Level 1 students into the spacious dining hall. The tables were arranged into Grade Levels, with three tables allocated to Level 1 students. Lily was already sitting at a table that was full, so Rachaya sat at an empty table instead.

'That girl, Lily,' said an attractive, dark-skinned girl. Rachaya recognised her as the one who had laughed at Reijko during Mr Thestral's speech. 'She's a water dragon. Friendly enough, but their minds flow and change as often as the current. They don't mean to be rude. Can I sit here?'

Grateful for the show of friendliness, Rachaya nodded and the girl sat down.

'I'm Naz. We're the only two fires in our dorm. You're Rachaya?'

'Yes.'

'The princess,' said Naz with a laugh. 'It'll be hard for you at first, not having grown up with other dragons.'

'Tell me about it,' muttered Rachaya.

'Ah well, don't worry about it. You'll pick it all up soon enough. Besides, I was here last year so I can help show you the ropes.'

Rachaya smiled gratefully.

'I like your cat. What's his name?'

'It's a she, and her name's Tibbles. I've had her since forever.'

'You're lucky. All I've ever had is a jub jub. Stupid birds. I'm sure your cat would make short work out of one of them,' Naz said.

'A jub jub?'

'Yep.' Seeing Rachaya's confusion, she added, 'Like a miniature oka, only much stupider. If such a thing is possible.'

Rachaya laughed, feeling much less nervous now she had met Naz.

They were interrupted by a teacher who had come waddling over to the table.

'Ah, Nazish,' said the large water dragon. Her double chins wobbled with each word. 'It's good to see you helping one of our newcomers.' The teacher ambled off to find her dinner, her body jiggling with each step.

'Mrs Watercress. Never remembers that I hate being called Nazish,' muttered Naz. 'You'll have her for Dragon Studies.'

'You won't be in Dragon Studies?' she asked.

'No, that's one of the subjects I'm doing at Level 2.'

'So you've really been at Wyvold's before?'

'Sure,' said Naz with a shrug.

'It's just that, for humans, we . . . I mean, they always go up a level at the beginning of every year.'

'Really? Even if they haven't built their skills up yet?'

Rachaya nodded.

'But then, how do they cope with the harder work?'

Rachaya shrugged. She'd never thought of it like that before 'I guess they don't.'

'But then they'd fall further and further behind.'

'I think humans think it will embarrass them if they're kept back a year.'

'What? There's nothing embarrassing about not being ready to advance. Everyone develops at a different rate. Surely even humans know that?'

'I guess not,' said Rachaya.

Their conversation was interrupted by a senior student who came around and filled up their plates with food. Every seat was soon occupied and conversations stopped as everyone shovelled food into their mouths. Even compared with the food at the castle the meal was good. They had tasty chicken and leek soup, followed by some sort of pie and vegetables (which Rachaya devoured greedily as they had not been present at Perfero Castle), and a generous piece of lemon meringue pie for dessert.

Once the meal was over, Naz took Rachaya on a tour of the school, showing her where each of the classrooms were on Rachaya's timetable. A burly gardener was pulling weeds out of the garden.

'He seems big, even for an earth dragon,' Rachaya said.

Naz frowned slightly. 'He must be new. He wasn't here last year. The gardener used to be Mr Peat, an old water dragon who blasted anyone with water from his fingertips if they stepped on his garden beds.'

Rachaya coloured in each of the rooms on her map so she would be able to find them again. The tour ended back at their dormitory, where Naz showed her the Level 1 lounge.

'We can come in here after Study,' Naz said. 'They give us milk and biscuits for supper. I think they do it because they feel bad about making us sit silently at our desks for an hour and a half each night.'

Rachaya dropped her map in surprise. 'An hour and a half,' she said, bending down to pick up her map. 'I don't think I can sit still for a whole hour and a half.'

'You get used to it. Besides, we are only supervised by Level 4 or Level 5 students. They will usually turn a blind eye to any note passing or whispers going on between the desks.'

The two girls went back to their dorm and sat on Rachaya's bed.

'The lounge is a great place to talk to the boys,' whispered Naz. 'I find them . . . nicer . . . than the girls. They're simpler.'

A great balloon of hope swelled in her belly as Rachaya went to bed that night. She was actually looking forward to her first full day of lessons now that she had met Naz.

CHAPTER 13

LESSONS BEGIN

Breakfast the next morning was an informal, serve-yourself meal before the students had to rush off to their first classes. For the Level 1 students this was Magical Education Theory. After learning what Mikel could do with magic, Rachaya had been looking forward to this subject. She walked into the classroom and stopped dead, causing a diminutive air dragon to crash into her. In every aspect the classroom was so unlike the room in her village school that Rachaya was almost certain she was in the wrong place.

Along the back wall of the classroom ran a series of shelves, each supporting a myriad of colourful and interesting objects. Rachaya wished she could look at them more closely. On a golden stand stood a glass orb. Inside the orb was a glowing, blue, almond-shaped eye that seemed to follow Rachaya as she moved about the room in search of a spare seat. Next to the orb was a stuffed alligator, standing upright and holding a spear in a clawed hand. It seemed oddly out of place among the rest of the artefacts. One of the glass jars seemed to be filled with a liquid metal. It was sitting on a rotating stand and as it spun the metal swooshed around in the jar. There were dozens of other jars and glass cases filled with liquids and strange objects.

Pinned all along one wall were posters of every size, shape and colour. One poster depicted the phases of Escoria's three moons. Another, which Rachaya especially liked, was a chart of a large oak tree with the twelve seasons written on it, one for each branch. Under each season was a list of the spells best suited to that time of year. The other posters outlined safety procedures, correct stance and body posture for different spell types, and lists of ways to identify different potion ingredients.

The third wall was all windows, allowing sunshine to spill into the classroom, making it seem friendly and inviting. The fourth wall held an enormous blackboard, in front of which was the teacher's desk.

Their teacher was Miss Hobstone, a pleasant young fire dragon with wire-rimmed glasses. Something about the teacher's kind face made Rachaya like her immediately. The students held on to Miss Hobstone's every word as the teacher explained that they would be learning the theory behind basic everyday magic, with a practical, hands-on lesson once a week in their different elemental groups.

'But don't expect to be able to do it all at once,' she warned the eager class. 'It takes years to be able to control the ebb and flow of magic, and most dragons will never be able to do more than the most basic of spells. Even those with a degree of talent for magic will never even come close to the skills possessed by the wizards.'

After an introduction to the subject, the students played some getting-to-know-you games. Afterward they had just enough time to carefully copy notes titled *What is Magic?* from the board into their crisp new notebooks before the bell sounded.

'You made a great start today, students,' Miss Hobstone called over the noise of students clambering to their feet. They headed off to their next class, Fire Studies.

Unlike Magical Education, where all the Level 1 students were together, only the fire dragons were in Fire Studies. There were only five students in the class: Rachaya and Naz, Morhol, and two other boys, Max and Shahann. Their teacher, Mr Cole, was a very serious fire dragon with an obvious passion for his subject. His classroom was hewn out of stone.

'So we don't burn down the entire school,' whispered Naz. A row of desks and benches had been carved out of the rock. A cushion had been placed on each seat, making the room a little bit more comfortable. Like Miss Hobstone, Mr Cole warned them all not to expect too much, too soon.

'You need to learn how to be safe with fire. Only then will you be allowed to try to cast your fire at will.'

Mr Cole placed mats along the ground and the students practised dropping and rolling around.

'This will be vital if your clothing catches on fire,' he explained to them all. 'As fire dragons, your body cannot burn, but it can be very uncomfortable if your clothing melts to your skin.'

The students had to go around the room locating all the fire-quenching equipment. The list was so long it trailed along the floor, and Rachaya kept tripping over it. She couldn't believe how many secret crevices had been carved into the rock for the sake of hiding safety equipment.

'Why didn't you just get a cupboard in the back of the room?' she asked Mr Cole.

'And what if that is where the fire is?' he retorted. He ran his fingers through his hair in exasperation. 'You will learn soon enough that fire is an unpredictable element and that we must take all possible precautions at all times. And, from what I've heard, Miss Perfero,' he added with a hint of sarcasm, 'you in particular need to learn to control your fire.'

As he walked away to speak to another student, Rachaya could have sworn she heard him mutter, 'She won't be burning down my school. Not on my watch.'

After a quick recess Rachaya had Hopology with the air dragons down in the Weaponry Dome.

'It's the study of the use of weapons,' Naz explained.

'Ooh, I've been looking forward to that,' Rachaya said. 'Is it as fun as it seems?'

'Sure, if you like getting hit in the head a lot, it's great.'

The classroom was even more interesting than she had expected. Hanging from the walls were swords, battleaxes, bows, knives, daggers and spears, as well as many other weapons that Rachaya had never seen before. Like the Magical Education classroom, there were also several posters hanging up on the walls. Most were diagrams of the correct combative stances, but one was a very gruesome chart outlining different injuries and how to treat them. Naz gulped when Rachaya pointed it out to her.

The brawny Level 1 coordinator, Mr Ruffhead, was their teacher. He was wearing tight-fitting clothing once again, making each and every one of his enormous muscles bulge out.

'You are all to wear tight-fitting clothing in the Weaponry Dome at all times,' he instructed the class. 'Loose clothing is a danger in here. There are too many weapons flying around, and believe me when I say you don't want to get your sleeve caught in one of them.' Rachaya hastily pulled off her enormous blazer.

Mr Ruffhead began the lesson by splitting the students into permanent working groups. To their disappointment Rachaya and Naz were separated into different groups. The surly Morhol was in Rachaya's group, as well as three tiny air dragons; a girl from her dorm, Raevyn, and two boys, Aethon and Reijko. The generally excitable air dragon smiled weakly at Rachaya, far from his usual, eager self. Rachaya sidled over to Morhol, so when Mr Ruffhead came around to their group he paired the two of them up.

'Although we may have to rearrange the partners a little bit later on,' said Mr Ruffhead with a grunt. 'Young Miss Perfero here seems no match for you in size, Morhol.'

Mr Ruffhead set them the task of sparring with blunt swords while he went around the room correcting stance and grip. He was immediately impressed with Rachaya and Morhol.

'We have two naturals here, I see,' he announced to the rest of the class, causing Rachaya to blush. 'Perhaps you two are more evenly matched than I thought.' He placed Rachaya's hands properly on the hilt. It felt unnatural to hold the sword like that but, by the end of the lesson, it felt more comfortable. Rachaya couldn't wait to tell Naz that she was actually good at something and she wondered how her friend was faring over in her own group. Rachaya saw no sign of her at the end of the lesson, so she hurried off to lunch on her own. There was still no sign of Naz in the dining hall, so she sat next to the terse Morhol instead.

'Thanks for pairing with me,' Rachaya said, taking some ham and beef sandwiches from a plate in the middle of the table. Morhol raised his dark eyebrows and smirked.

'Like you gave me a choice,' he said.

'I just thought we could be friends,' she replied.

For some reason, that made him angry.

'I see,' he spat. 'You're think a street rat you caught stealing food and who has a disgraced mother would be desperate for friends. I suppose from the lofty heights of the castle a princess is taught how to look for a charity case.'

Rachaya looked him square in the eyes. 'Actually, no-one here has mentioned your mother, or referred to you as a "street rat". My cousin, Mikel, told me you would also be a new student at Wyvolds when we saw you at my Coronation Carnival. Since then you were the only familiar face I knew who would be at my new school. And, for the record, my father is a butcher *and* a human, and he's the best parent ever, so who am I to judge anyone else's?' She went to leave, but stopped when Morhol laughed.

'I think we'll get along just fine, Princess,' he said. He took an enormous bite of sandwich meat, the bread discarded, and gave her a huge smile, causing kangaroo meat to cascade from his mouth.

'Pig,' she muttered as she sat back down and took a bite out of her beef sandwich.

Morhol swallowed. 'No, kangaroo,' he said. His shoulders relaxed and he began to explain to her some of the ins and outs of being a dragon. He warned her that many of the students would gossip about her because she was new to the island.

'But I wouldn't worry too much,' he said. 'People have been gossiping about me my whole life and I've turned out okay.'

When Naz still hadn't shown up by the end of lunch, Morhol waited for Rachaya to collect her books from her dorm for their next class – Personal Development. They headed to class together in companionable silence. There they found Naz sporting a swollen eye.

'Sword in the face and me, the most experienced one there,' she said with a laugh. 'I'm Naz by the way,' she said to Morhol.

Upon entering the room they realised that, once again, there were only fire dragons in this class. Their teacher, Mrs Byrne, bustled into the room and dropped a pile of books and stationery on her desk. Several items clattered to the floor but she didn't seem to notice. She combed a stray hair behind her ear, releasing around seven more in the process. She looked decidedly frazzled.

'The biggest challenge for fire dragons,' she said without preamble, 'is controlling our tempers. In this class we will practise meditation, the art of thinking before we act and the skill of blocking our minds from unwanted visitors.'

She walked up to each of the five students and touched them on the forehead, nodding thoughtfully as she did so. When it was her turn Rachaya jolted in surprise – it had felt unpleasant, like the teacher had zapped her.

'I can see this class is no different from any other Personal Development class I have taught. You all have fiery tempers bubbling close to the surface.' The class laughed and Mrs Byrne turned severe. 'Lose your temper and the enemy wins. Always remember that. Although dragons have been at peace for many years, the other elemental groups know of our weakness and will happily exploit it if they can. And so, on to meditation.'

She instructed Max and Shahann to place five mats on the floor. As they placed each one she fretfully straightened them.

'Pick a mat and sit on it,' she told the class once she was happy with the mats. Once the students were seated she sat on her own mat. Rachaya watched as Mrs Byrne lifted her left leg up and forced it to rest on top of her right leg. Her movements were slow and stiff, and her bones creaked with the effort. 'You should be sitting thus,' she called out to the class waving her arms about to draw attention to her painfully placed legs. Rachaya copied the teacher, her younger bones finding it an easier position to rest in than the teacher's.

'Now close your eyes and imagine you are floating along on a fluffy cloud.'

To her left Rachaya heard Morhol choke on his laughter, and Rachaya suddenly found it very difficult not to laugh herself.

'You are floating on this cloud, allowing its tendrils of moisture to wash all of your anger away.'

Rachaya took in several deep breaths, gulping down the giggles that were threatening to escape her throat.

'Swishhhhh. Swissshhhhhh,' said Mrs Byrne. It was too much. Rachaya barked out a shout of laughter. Morhol and Naz joined her and very soon the entire class were rolling around on the floor in fits of giggles. Mrs Byrne sighed and shook her head.

'Every year, the same thing,' she said once the class was quiet once more. 'Rachelle, I expect better from you.' Rachaya looked around, confused. Who was this 'Rachelle'? The other students seemed just as perplexed.

Giving up on meditation for the time being, Mrs Byrne decided to test their skills of mind shielding. She went around the room trying to force her way into each student's mind in turn.

'Well done, Edalbert,' the teacher said to Naz. 'Very good for a first time.'

'I was here last year. I've done this loads of times,' said Naz through gritted teeth.

'Were you, dear?' Mrs Byrne asked, fluttering her hands in that strange, distracted way of hers. 'Well, well. That's good.'

She moved on to Morhol. Naz shook her head in disbelief.

'She never remembers the students' names,' Naz whispered. 'I'd hoped she would at least recognise my face this year though.'

Mrs Byrne continued to flutter about the room, trying to achieve everything while succeeding at nothing.

'Wait, class, I forgot to set your homework,' she cried out when the bell rang to signal the end of the period. 'Most unlike me. I'm usually much more organised that this.' She began to mutter incoherently to herself.

'What's the homework?' asked Morhol. Mrs Byrne jumped.

'What? Oh, yes, the homework.' She straightened herself up and rubbed her palm vigorously across her forehead. 'Please complete a nightly thought diary, to be checked by me each week. Just write whatever springs to mind on a page or two in your notebooks. It's easier to block something when you're aware it's there, if that makes sense?'

'Ya huh,' said Naz, eyebrows raised. When Mrs Byrne made no further comment the students filed out of the room.

'Last year I used Personal Development to catch up on my sleep,' Naz said as they headed up to the Level 1 lounge. 'Mrs Byrne never remembers who any of us are, so what's the point?'

'Are you sure, Edalbert? She really seemed to like you,' Rachaya said with a wink.

'She sure did.' Naz laughed. 'What sort of name is Edalbert anyway?'

The student lounge was bubbling with excitement when they entered it. While they were in class someone had pinned sign-up sheets for weekly recreational activities to the wall. Rachaya pushed her way through the crowd of water dragons that blocked her view and scanned the sheets. The Hopology Club most excited Rachaya, but one look at Naz's black and swollen eye convinced her not to even suggest it.

'How about Oka Handling?' she called out to Naz and Morhol. 'You can use my oka.'

'I don't mind, so long as the three of us are together,' said Naz. Morhol nodded his agreement, so Rachaya wrote their names down for the activity.

They grabbed a handful of biscuits each and headed back out to the school grounds. Naz led them around to where each of Morhol's classes were, just as she had done for Rachaya the day before.

'That's the farmlands up there,' she pointed out behind the main office building. 'All of our fruit comes from the orchards, and our vegetables and wheat come from the farmlands. All the students get to help with the harvest at the end of the year.'

'So we're slaves now?' Morhol asked.

'No, it's fun. And you get to eat as you go, which is great if you don't mind fruit. Last year I ate so many cherries I threw up.'

The trio explored the lake and landing field, Weaponry Dome, armoury, greenhouses and oka stables. Rachaya couldn't believe how large the school was.

'My human school was only a single room in the centre of the village,' she told the others. 'And we only had classes in the afternoon.'

'What did you do in the mornings?'

'We worked for our parents. I used to help my father at his butcher shop.'

'No wonder you're stronger than you look,' Morhol said, impressed.

Rachaya wondered how she would ever remember where everything was. She lost her bearings and was surprised when they ended up in the dining hall.

'I thought the dining hall was over there,' she said to the others, pointing out into the growing darkness. Morhol and Naz laughed at her as they walked across the room to their seats.

'I think we'll have to get your school map framed for you. You're definitely going to need it,' said Morhol. They had entered via a different door than the previous night and had to walk past the different Grade Levels to get to the Level 1 tables.

'Oi, Hektor, isn't that your cousin?' shouted a blond, freckle-faced boy as they passed the Level 4 tables.

'So she says,' shouted Hektor with a sneer. 'Although my mother and I don't believe it. I'm not even sure she's really a dragon.'

Rachaya quickly turned away. Her heart quickened and blood pounded in her ears.

Naz gripped her arm. 'Just ignore him. Everyone's watching. Smile and pretend you didn't hear,' she hissed. Rachaya nodded and allowed her friends to steer her to the Level 1 tables. Everyone soon got bored with watching them when they saw that Rachaya was not going to react.

'I bet he was annoyed when you showed up, knocking him off the throne,' Morhol said between noisy slurps of his soup.

'You could say that. He forbade me from ever speaking with him or his friends.'

Naz snorted into her bowl. 'He did what? You outrank him you know. As if he can ever forbid or order you to do anything.'

'I've never thought of it like that before,' Rachaya said thoughtfully. She picked up her spoon and began to eat, determined not to let Hektor bother her.

After dinner the students had their first ever Study session. Rachaya filled in her thought diary in no time, just writing down whatever nonsense popped into her head. No other teacher had set them homework yet, so she spent the rest of the session writing a letter to her father. She knew he would want to hear all about her new friends and how she was settling in.

'Ouch!' she said when something hit her on the temple. She looked around for the cause and saw a crumpled piece of paper. She looked up and saw Naz grinning at her.

'Open it,' she mouthed. Rachaya opened the note.

'RACHELLE!' was all the note said. Rachaya smiled.

'EDALBERT!' she wrote back and threw the note onto Naz's desk.

'If I see any notes I will have no choice but to confiscate them,' called out the Level 4 student supervising them. Naz pulled a silly face and hid the note. Rachaya smiled down into her desk. She would describe Mrs Byrne to her father, too. That should give him a laugh or two.

CHAPTER 14

ZEB, THE FLYING WATER DRAGON

By the time she and her friends had made their way down to breakfast the next morning the entire school had heard about Hektor and his taunts that Rachaya was not a real dragon. The response of the students was divided; those who liked Hektor made a show of disliking or ignoring Rachaya. Those who didn't like Hektor – and there seemed to be an awful lot of people in this category – went out of their way to be friendly toward Rachaya.

'I don't know why you're surprised,' Morhol said through a mouthful of scrambled egg. 'You're next in line to the throne, whereas he's now a nobody. Unless you die, of course.'

'Morhol! That's a horrible thing to say,' Naz said, landing a punch on his arm with a *thud*. Morhol didn't even flinch.

Morhol shrugged. 'It's what everyone's thinking.'

'Even I'm thinking it,' admitted Rachaya.

Rachaya felt as if there were many pairs of eyes staring at her as she and her friends made their way to their first class for the day. She had Transformation. This was what she had been really looking forward to – learning how to transform into a dragon.

'Have you transformed yet?' she asked Naz.

'Only once. I can't seem to do it again. That's why they kept me in Level 1.'

'Really? I thought it was because you can't make it through a Hopology lesson without breaking your nose?' Morhol said.

'And I thought it was because you can't stop giggling in Personal Development,' Rachaya chipped in innocently. Naz hit them both good-naturedly on the arm.

'You'll see. It's not as easy as it looks,' she said.

Transformation took place in a small classroom by the lake. All Level 1 students were in the class, and every single chair in the room was taken up. The only other items in the room were a small blackboard and a teacher's desk.

'I know it's a little cramped in here. But,' their teacher, the kooky Mrs Stacey explained, 'we will spend most of our time outdoors. It's no good having you all transform inside a classroom. Only we air dragons would be able to fit!'

The students' first task was to complete yet another getting-to-know-you activity, so Naz led them over to Reijko, who was standing with a chubby, square-faced boy with an endearing smile. Naz gave the large boy a friendly tap on the arm.

'How's it going, Zeb?' she asked. 'You're back in Level 1, too?'

'I didn't want to be separated from you and your tough love.'

Naz laughed. 'This is Rachaya and Morhol. Guys, this is Zhabiib, but everyone calls him Zeb.'

'Hello,' Zeb said cheerfully. 'Have you all met Reijko?' He motioned toward the tiny pale-faced boy. Reijko nodded politely to Rachaya, Naz and Morhol.

As a group, they had to complete a Who's-Who? chart, answering questions such as where people had gone on holiday recently, what their favourite dessert was, and whether they had any pets. Naz and Zeb had already done this the year before so they turned it into a great joke. The others soon joined in.

'I don't mind you joking and laughing,' said Mrs Stacey. 'It's clear you are getting to know each other like I asked. But please keep it down to a dull roar, okay?'

Rachaya discovered that it was Zeb's greatest dream to be able to fly.

'But aren't you a water dragon?' she asked the dreamy-faced boy. 'I didn't think you lot could fly.'

Zeb's face fell a little. 'We can't,' he admitted. 'Not usually, anyway. But we have wings. We use them to propel ourselves through the water. I'm sure they could be used to fly.'

One of the earth-dragon boys on the table behind them had been eavesdropping on the conversation, and now he snorted in disbelief.

'Do ya hear that, Aodfin?' he said to a boy with dreadlocks and enormous muscles. 'That boy wants to *fly*.'

Aodfin shrugged his massive shoulders and refused to join his two companions in their sniggering. 'If he wants to try to fly so be it,' he said in a deep, commanding voice. 'That's not our concern. We need to finish this activity. So tell me, have you ever gone on holiday to the Nomad Wastelands? If you have I need to know so I can write your name in this square.'

The other two earth dragons begrudgingly returned to their work, leaving Zeb alone.

Morhol looked thoughtful. 'Do you know what?' he said, sure the earth dragons were no longer listening to their conversation. 'I reckon you could fly, with the help of a little magic. My mum was telling me that dragons can learn to levitate in their human forms. What if they can in their dragon forms, too?'

'Really? You think so?'

'Sure, leave it with me,' Morhol told Zeb. He winked at Rachaya. At that moment, Mrs Stacey called the class to attention, and they spent the rest of the lesson writing notes and discussing 'What is Transformation?'.

Naz noticed Rachaya rubbing her sore wrist. 'Don't worry, it's not normally like this,' she whispered. 'Once we have all of the notes down we spend most of the lesson out on the lawn trying to transform. It's great fun.'

After lunch the Level 1 students had Gemology. Rachaya discovered very quickly that this would be her least favourite subject. Their teacher, Miss Upton, was an overweight, elderly earth dragon who stomped sullenly into the classroom. She wrote the page and question numbers on the board, barked 'Get to work!' at the students, plonked down into her seat and promptly fell asleep. After a few minutes some of the students began to muck around. Up woke Miss Upton Hell hath no fury like an up-woken Miss Upton! She raged at them for a full ten minutes, calling them rude and ignorant upstarts. She was puffing and panting from the effort by the time she was through with them. She lowered herself feebly into her chair and within seconds had fallen back to sleep.

'What was that?' Rachaya mouthed.

'That's just what she does,' Naz mouthed back with a shrug.

The students remained silent for the rest of the lesson. Once they had completed the work Rachaya and Naz played noughts and crosses on the back page of Naz's notebook, but they soon became bored. Even staring at the beautiful gems that lay on velvet cushions in glass cabinets around the room lost its charm after a while.

'What in the known lands of Escoria was that?' Morhol said once they were safely out of Gemology. 'Is she even allowed to teach like that?'

'It's not really teaching though, is it?' Rachaya said. 'I've never been so bored in my entire life.'

'Well, get used to it. It's like that every lesson,' Naz said. 'I'm sure I only failed that subject last year because it was so dull. For some reason the school won't get rid of her. I think she's friends with Mr Thestral or something. Apparently they started off teaching together so he lets her get away with anything.'

Recreation wasn't due to start for several weeks so the students had some spare time before dinner. Rachaya, Naz and Morhol went to the student lounge where they met up with Zeb. Reijko was with him.

'Do you mind if Reijko hangs out with us for a bit? The only other dragons here are earths,' Zeb asked.

Reijko shuddered. 'Some of them can be a bit . . . tetchy,' he said, his grey eyes open as wide as they could go. 'That's why I prefer to spend my time with the other races. Aodfin's not too bad, but his friends can be a bit mean.'

'They're the boys who were laughing at Zeb in Transformation?'

'Yep. Carswell and Drakan. I'd stay well clear of them if I were you. But Aodfin would never let them go too far.'

Rachaya nodded. If there had been a voice of reason like Aodfin in Cryll she might not have been tied up to the stake by the villagers. She told Reijko this, and he seemed shocked to hear of the trouble she'd had.

'Yes, but they didn't know that I was a princess,' she joked.

'Are you a princess?' Reijko asked innocently. Everyone started laughing, confusing Reijko further. He waited for them to calm down, a patient look on his face.

'Haven't you heard the gossip?' Naz wiped the tears of laughter from her eyes. 'It's been all over Fyrebyrne Island.'

'No.'

'Rachaya here is a princess, showing up out of the blue to oust old Prince Mikel from being second in line to the throne.'

'Ah.' Reijko nodded. 'That explains why Hektor is being even more unpleasant than usual.'

Once again, eyes followed Rachaya as she joined the rest of the school for dinner. She didn't mind so much now that she had a group of friends by her side.

Rachaya gradually settled in to life at Wyvolds and by the end of the week felt ready to explore further. So on Moonsday afternoon Naz took her down to the local village for the first time. It was made up of a small, sleepy collection of cottages. The streets were paved with cobblestones, along which ran jub jubs, the miniature version of the wingless oka only twice as brainless, pecking in between the cracks in search of food. The village was very pretty, with well-kept gardens and lush green yards – far more pleasant than the dusty streets of her human village.

Once the two girls had looked in the windows of all the shops they settled down in a cafe and bought themselves an ice-cream each. Rachaya had never seen some of the flavours before. Although there was the usual chocolate, strawberry and vanilla, there was also lamb, blood and jub jub flavoured.

'Do dragons really enjoy eating these?' asked Rachaya, wrinkling up her nose at the thought.

'Only the more militant dragons. It's usually earth dragons that would eat meat flavoured ice-cream or sweets. They're mad for their meat. Air dragons are either vegetarian or insectivorous, though, so they'd stick to the sesame seed or black poppy ice-creams.'

Rachaya chose a chocolate ice-cream and the girls sat out the front of the cafe in the afternoon sunshine. Rachaya nearly dropped her ice-cream when Naz reached out and grabbed her arm tightly.

'What's he up to?' Naz hissed.

'Who?'

'*Morhol*. Look!' Naz pointed to a shadowy figure creeping along the edge of a building. Morhol's thick eyebrows were pulled down in a frown and his eyes were darting all over the place. He had a long cloak on over his school uniform. As they watched, Morhol placed one hand on the latch of a shop door and looked about. He gave a guilty start when he caught sight of Naz and Rachaya. He abandoned his quest and walked over to them.

'What are you two doing here?' he asked.

'I think we have more reason to be asking that, what with you creeping about like you're on a heist or something,' Naz said. 'What are you up to?'

'If you must know I was trying to help Zeb,' he said in exasperation. 'You know, to fly.'

'Ah,' said Naz, comprehension dawning.

Rachaya watched the two of them, completely at a loss as to what her two friends were talking about. Naz laughed when she noticed Rachaya's startled expression. Rachaya looked down and saw with dismay that, in her curiosity, she had let the ice-cream melt all down her arm. Naz passed her a handkerchief to clean herself up.

She wiped her arm clean. 'So are you two going to tell me what you're going on about?' she asked.

'Morhol here was going to go into the Wizard Shop. You can buy simple magical solutions to everyday problems from the wizards. But,' she added darkly, 'it isn't the done thing.'

'Why not?'

'Are you serious?' Naz said. 'Firstly, wizards are evil, conniving beasts. And secondly, most dragons consider it to be cheating. You know, getting a quick fix for something that can be achieved yourself with a little bit of effort. Oh, and not to mention that performing non-dragon magic is completely illegal. Things can go badly for you if people see you enter a Wizard Shop.'

'But I need to try to help Zeb, and I really don't know what else I can do,' Morhol said with frustration.

'Zeb's our friend, too,' Rachaya said. 'We'll all go in together. Besides, I'd like to see one of these shops. It could be interesting.'

Naz rolled her eyes but said nothing. The three of them waited until no-one else was around. When the entire street was empty they dashed across the road and launched themselves into the shop.

If Rachaya had thought that the stores run by dragons were strange, they were nothing compared with the Wizard Shop. It was dark and dingy, making it difficult to see, and a heavy perfume clung to the air making their brains feel dull and heavy. The whole store – walls, shelves, floor, everything – was lined with faded blue velvet. Perched on the shelves was dust-coated bric-a-brac, the sort of items everyone except little old ladies would throw away.

'The wizards use them to make amulets,' Morhol told Rachaya in a muffled voice.

Behind the counter stood a hunchbacked old man, far older than anyone Rachaya had ever met before. His skin was wrinkled and translucent and his large bottom lip quivered, making his wispy silver beard wobble. He surveyed the trio with pale, icy eyes that lay beneath two large, bristly eyebrows.

'Red hair,' he squawked, exposing a row of crooked yellow teeth.

'Sorry?' said Rachaya nervously.

'Red hair. Perfero red hair. What would the princess want with magic, hmmm? A protective amulet to ward off her enemies? Or perhaps something a little more *sinister*?'

'Actually, it's me who wanted to look at some magic,' Morhol said bravely, placing himself under the wizard's scrutiny.

'Oh you are, are you?' asked the wizard. He let out a croaking, cackling laugh. 'And you brought two girls in to protect you, did you, boy?'

Morhol clenched his fists in anger but made no response. Naz let out an angry growl.

'We did not come here to trade insults,' she said angrily. 'Will you help our friend or not?'

The wizard stepped out from behind the counter and came at them with surprising speed. He seemed to grow larger with each step he took and power swirled around the room, knocking objects off the overladen shelves.

'Let me make one thing clear to you, children. Magic is a privilege a wizard sometimes chooses to share. And I choose not to share with spoiled little brats. Now get out of my store before I turn you all into rats. Brats into rats . . . Yes, I'd like that.' He raised his arms above his head and the students bolted. Once they were safely several streets away from the store they stopped to catch their breath.

'That wizard was mental!' Morhol puffed.

'I tried to tell you. *That's* why you never meddle with wizards,' Naz said. 'First they stole our freedom, and then they taunt us. I hate them.'

'But what about Zeb?' Rachaya asked.

'I'll think of a way,' Morhol said. 'There's always another way.'

***

The weather may never change on Fyrebyrne Island, but the weeks flew by none the less. As she settled into the routine at Wyvolds, Rachaya began to discover her strengths and weaknesses. Even though she wasn't even close to transforming yet, Rachaya had found that she was quite good at Practical Magic. She felt an odd thrill in the pit of her stomach the first time she had successfully used a lost and found spell to locate the shoe Morhol had hidden.

'Excellent, Rachaya,' Miss Hobstone had said. 'The further away the object is the weaker the signal, so now practise moving the shoe further away.'

The thought of it made Rachaya smile for a full three days.

She continued to improve in Hopology, remained bored in Gemology, and was consistently giggly with Naz in Personal Development. In Dragon Studies, the students started to learn how to speak in Dragon Tongue, translating directly from Common Tongue. Rachaya had to admit that this was her hardest subject, and she struggled to get her tongue around the odd, harsh sounds. They also learnt the history of the dragons. Rachaya found this very interesting and learnt a lot about her mother's family. She also enjoyed Herbalism, even though she found it difficult to tell the difference between the plants. It had been a long time since her mother had taught her in their garden at home. Their teacher, Mr Hopp, had been Adara's teacher, too.

'You're the very image of her,' he told Rachaya during their first lesson. 'I know I can expect good things from you. Your mother was especially good at herbalism.'

Herbalism wasn't just growing and identifying plants. It also involved making healing brews, and Rachaya loved brewing the potions. She may have needed Naz's good eye for discerning the plants, but she was good at cooking with them.

All in all, Rachaya already loved Wyvolds and was very glad that Mikel had found her and brought her to Fyrebyrne Island. Hektor continued to be unpleasant, snubbing Rachaya at every opportunity and voicing his doubts as to her parentage as loud as he could every chance he had. But Rachaya found she wasn't bothered by Hektor. She had friends and allies, something she never hoped for on Fyrebyrne Island after Lady Anjela's stony welcome. An enemy was much easier to ignore when you had friends to get annoyed on your behalf.

CHAPTER 15

A CURE FOR BAMBOO

'Today's lesson is not for the faint of heart,' said Miss Hobstone, their Magical Education teacher, who was sitting carelessly on the edge of her desk. They were in their weekly practical class, so the only students present were the five Level 1 fire dragons. Miss Hobstone looked at them seriously over her thin wire spectacles. 'It's not for the feeble-minded, either. Today we are beginning basic healing magic. The first thing to remember is this: if you are not one hundred per cent certain that you can heal a person, go and get someone who can. Healing magic is not to be taken lightly, nor should you ever just give it a go and hope it will all turn out for the best.

'But,' she said, flashing them a winning smile, 'because our patients for today will be this array of bamboo sticks, I am sure you will all be fine.'

Rachaya, who had been holding her breath, let out a sigh of relief. Although she was fine at her father's butcher shop, she wasn't certain she would be able to deal with blood on something living.

'First, we need to create a wound that we can heal.' The teacher picked up one of the pieces of bamboo and a sharp knife. She slashed across the thick skin, revealing the plant's fleshy insides. 'Now, this is a nice, clean cut. Much easier to heal that an uneven gash. We will begin with clean wounds and move on to more complicated injuries when you are all ready.' She placed the knife back down on her desk.

'So now that we have our wound we need to heal it. Place your hand over it like this, disgusting as that may be with some cuts.'

The class laughed weakly. Rachaya looked at Naz and wrinkled her nose.

'Is it as disgusting as it looks?' she whispered. Naz nodded in reply and grinned at her. Rachaya groaned. Looking around the room, she wasn't the only student who was feeling queasy. Morhol's face had turned pale, and Max and Shahann were looking at the teacher with horror. Only Naz seemed unperturbed. Miss Hobstone shushed them and went back to her demonstration.

'Now, delve down in your mind and place your thoughts on to the wound, much as you would if you wanted to thought-speak with the bamboo. If you do this properly you should be able to feel each individual cellulose fibre within your inner mind. Pluck these fibres with your mind and knit them together, using your magic to hold them in place. And there we go! A cured plant.'

She held the stick of bamboo up to show the class. The students all clapped when they saw the flawless stick of bamboo.

'Okay, class, now it's your turn.' Miss Hobstone gave them an encouraging smile. 'Select a piece of bamboo and carefully slice it. Deeper than that, Shahann. Once you have made your cut go back to your desks and try to heal your plant. And I will have silence, please. This will require your full concentration. Oh, and Nazish, you can do a crosshatch weave for today as you've already mastered the basics.'

Rachaya joined the queue to get her bamboo stick. She sliced it the way she saw Miss Hobstone cut her plant earlier and carried it carefully back to her desk. She placed her hand over the neat cut. It felt slightly sticky, and she tried not to think of blood. She felt really stupid trying to delve down into her mind. It sounded just like something Mrs Byrne would tell them to do. Rachaya looked around the room and saw that everyone else was taking the exercise very seriously. Morhol had his eyes closed and she decided to try the same.

Once her eyes were closed Rachaya found it much easier to concentrate. She tried to delve down in her brain. Her mind started to thrum and she felt as if she were falling. She jolted in her seat and nearly slammed down into her desk. Rachaya squeezed her eyes closed even tighter and forced herself to keep concentrating. Her mind sailed downward until it hit something hard and slightly sticky. Rachaya searched about wildly in the darkness but couldn't find any cellulose fibres. Why couldn't she find any fibres? Perhaps if she tried shooting a little of her magic into it? But how would she do that? Rachaya imagined that she was sending magic down her arm and through her hand. She gasped when she felt some strands of bamboo in her mind. It was almost as if each individual cell was visible to her. She imagined she was weaving them together. The fibres moved beneath her hand, creating a sensation like ants crawling around under her skin. It tingled and itched. Rachaya ignored it for as long as she could, but then it was no use. She had to itch. She pulled her hand away and scratched vigorously at the phantom ants.

Miss Hobstone, seeing Rachaya had thrown aside her stick, came over to her and held up her bamboo. Rachaya's heart sank when she saw the plant. A jagged scar stood out starkly against the darker green, unmarked outer layer. In the centre there was a slight gap where the fleshy insides could still be seen.

'This is a fantastic first attempt, Rachaya,' Miss Hobstone said quietly. 'You have managed to locate the cellulose fibres very nicely. Go and grab a new stick and give it another go.' Miss Hobstone smiled reassuringly at Rachaya, and she felt a bubble of pride well up inside her. She went up to the teacher's desk and sliced open another piece of bamboo.

As Rachaya walked back to her desk she snuck a peek at the other students' work. Naz, who had obviously done this exercise before, had three perfectly healed pieces of bamboo sitting on her desk. Only the thinnest scar could be seen on each. Morhol was still working on his first piece. As he pulled his hand away from the bamboo Rachaya saw a dark, jagged scar across the middle, similar to her own attempt. She gave him the thumbs up as she sat down. Max and Shahann were still working on their first pieces, concentration etched across their faces. Max had gone red in the face, and Shahann was sweating.

Rachaya continued to heal sticks of bamboo, each scar thinner and neater than the one before. It was exhausting work, though, and she felt as if she had run a marathon by the time the bell rang to signal the end of class. She waved her friends on ahead of her so that she could finish off the last one.

'Well done today,' Miss Hobstone said with a kind smile as Rachaya left the room.

Rachaya returned the teacher's smile. 'Thanks, Miss Hobstone,' she said, closing the classroom door behind her.

Reijko was waiting for Rachaya outside the Magical Education classroom and asked if he could talk to her in private.

'Sure.' She led him to a deserted seating area nearby.

'Do you know what augury is?' he asked as they sat down on a bench under a tree.

'No,' she admitted. 'Is it a sort of board game? The one you showed Naz last Firesday?'

'No, it's even more exciting than that,' said Reijko. 'It's the study of the mystical world. It's part of the air-dragon curriculum. We learn how to read the future.'

'Oh, okay,' said Rachaya with a half-smile, not quite sure where he was going with this.

'Today we were discussing dreams. I had a dream about you.'

'About me?'

'Yes, and I described my dream to Mr Pennycuik, although I didn't tell him who my dream was about. Rachaya, he turned very white in the face. He even seemed to be trembling.' Reijko paused, trembling himself. 'He said that my dream was a strong indication that the person I dreamed of is in grave danger. Very grave danger. We're never supposed to tell people what we see about them when we walk in the dreamscape.' He reached out and clasped Rachaya's hands with his own. 'Very often what we see is just a sign of what *could* be, not what *will* be, but I had to warn you. Please, be careful.'

'Of a dream?'

'No. There is never anything to fear in a dream. It's the real world you must be wary of. Just be careful of your safety. Don't do anything stupid and think very carefully about the possible consequences for all your actions. Sorry I can't tell you more than that. Listen to your gut. Your instincts are almost always correct.'

Rachaya didn't know what to say so she thanked Reijko for his concern and suggested that they go up to lunch. He had been so earnest she couldn't get his warning out of her mind for the rest of the day. That night, as they sat on their beds in their dorm chatting, Rachaya asked Naz if air dragons could really predict the future.

'Well they say they can, and sometimes they can be scarily accurate. But I think they mostly just say vague words that people add their own meaning to.'

'And only air dragons have this skill?'

'Yes,' Naz said slowly. 'Air dragons have strong psychic powers, that's true. And earth dragons have enormous strength and water dragons can breathe under water. But some dragons are different to the rest. A few earth dragons, for example, can breathe fire, but not many can. A few fire dragons have been known to be super strong, but most aren't.'

'Why are a few dragons different? That doesn't seem right.'

'No-one really knows,' Naz said thoughtfully. 'But my guess is that we all originally came from the one type of dragon. My money would be on the sun dragons, although most people will tell you that they never existed.'

'My father told me a bit about them. He said they were supposed to be more powerful than all other dragons combined. Imagine that!' Rachaya said.

'Did he? Most dragons put them in the category of "mythological creature". In the old stories they were the true rulers of Escoria, and when they disappeared we descended into anarchy. A bitter war started between the dragon species around the time sun dragons were last reported to have been seen. What does Mikel think?'

'Mikel said they were just a myth, but I don't know. Why would my mum mention them to my dad if they were just a myth?'

Naz snorted with laughter. 'Probably just to scare the pants off him.'

The two girls sat quietly, each lost in their own thoughts.

'Hey!' Rachaya said after a while. 'You never said. What's our special power?'

'Well, obviously we can fly, we can command fire and,' she added with a laugh, 'we are, by far, better than every other species.'

'Except sun dragons.'

'Yes, except for them. But they're just a myth, I'm sure. And don't go around actually saying we're superior. The others don't seem to like it.'

'Miss Hobstone was saying that only air and fire dragons have the power of flight. So why does Zeb want to learn?'

'I don't know,' Naz said. 'Maybe he senses deep down that he has the power. Or maybe he's just crazy.'

'Shh,' Raevyn said, the tiny air dragon in their dorm.

'Anyway, why'd you want to know all this?' whispered Naz once Raevyn had gone back to her book. Rachaya told her about Reijko's predictions. Naz snorted again.

'You're not seriously worried, are you? I mean, Reijko means well but he's just a kid. I doubt if he could predict so much as what we're having for dinner tomorrow night.'

Naz's scoffing made Rachaya feel a little better and, as she lay in bed that night with Tibbles purring softly beside her, she decided not to let Reijko's dreams trouble her own.

The following Starsday Tibbles woke Rachaya at dawn by placing a soggy moth on her pillow. Seeing Naz was fast asleep, Rachaya decided to head down to the stables to visit Nyssa, her cheek still sticky from the moth. She had been able to push Reijko's warning completely out of her mind, but as she crossed the landing lawn it came screaming back to her. A gigantic water dragon came barrelling toward her. Rachaya dove out of the way just in time, landing hard on the ground and knocking the wind right out of her. A dark shadow loomed over her and she started to scream. A hand clamped firmly over her mouth.

'What's wrong with you?' came Morhol's familiar voice. 'It's just me.'

Rachaya struggled to sit up and saw Zeb morphing back into his human form.

'Why did you try to run me down?' she demanded once Morhol had removed his hand from her mouth.

'I didn't,' said Zeb, his usually cheerful face puckered with concern. 'I wasn't expecting anyone to come across the lawn so early. I was just trying to get a good run up.'

Rachaya raised her eyebrows, lost for words.

'I was going to take a huge leap,' Zeb explained. 'Morhol thinks that, if I go fast enough, I might be able to gain enough momentum to glide through the air for a bit. That's a little like flying, don't you think?'

'Why don't you use magic to keep yourself up in the air?' suggested Rachaya, thinking about the Wizard Shop. Drakan and Carswell stepped out from behind the bushes, clutching their sides from laughter. They must have been watching Zeb the whole time.

'Did I hear you right, freak?' Carswell sneered. 'You really think a reject like you, with paddles for wings, can fly?'

'And you, carrot top? You really think he is smart enough to use magic? A loser like that?' Drakan added.

'You watch your mouth,' Morhol said in a coldly quiet voice. He moved slightly to stand in front of Rachaya and Zeb, protecting them with his body.

'Yeah, and what are you gonna do about it, gutter boy?' Drakan asked. Morhol moved so fast Rachaya nearly missed it. He landed a cracking punch on Drakan's bulbous nose. A stunned expression spread across the earth dragon's stupid face before he passed out. Carswell threw himself at Morhol, pinning him to the ground. A shout sounded from the other side of the landing lawn as Aodfin came running. He pulled Carswell off Morhol.

'What in Escoria is wrong with you?' he roared.

'He punched Drakan,' Carswell whined, struggling to break free from Aodfin's iron grip.

'Drakan deserved it,' Rachaya shouted. 'You both came along and started insulting us all.'

'What do you think my father would say if he heard of this?' Aodfin asked Carswell, so quietly Rachaya was sure she wasn't supposed to hear.

'He won't.'

'If it had been a teacher who had spotted you he most definitely would have heard about it.' Aodfin turned to Rachaya and her friends. 'I'm sorry about this. You have my word that it won't happen again.' His muscles bulged as he hoisted Carswell over one shoulder, Drakan over the other, and trudged back to the dormitory building.

Morhol let out a low whistle. 'Now there's a dragon I'd rather fight beside than against,' he said.

'It looks like the rumours are true then,' Zeb said.

'What rumours?'

'That Aodfin's father has told him to look out for you at school. His dad was friends with your mum or something.'

'I think I've met his father once, the day I came to the island. Three gigantic earth dragons came to meet us when we landed. The leader of the group looked a lot like Aodfin.'

'Yeah, that would have been him,' said Morhol. 'Aodfin's father is the unofficial leader of the earth dragons. It's said that both Aodfin and his father have magical strength, far more than the other earths. You've made a powerful ally there.'

They headed in to breakfast together, all looking decidedly rumpled after such an action-packed morning.

'Thanks for sticking up for us,' Rachaya said once they had taken their seats.

Morhol shrugged.

'It's what friends do,' he said. He stuffed his mouth full of scrambled eggs, preventing any further conversation.

'Do you really think magic can help me fly?' asked Zeb, hope written all over his face.

'Sure, why not? In fire dragon classes we were told that most dragons need magic for long distance flights anyway, so we should be able to do it without resorting to wizards' tricks.' She shot a meaningful glance at Morhol. 'I can look into it for you.'

'Thanks.' Zeb smiled for the first time since he had nearly run her down that morning.

After they ate, Rachaya found Naz and dragged her to the magic section of the library. They pulled books off the shelf at random and flicked through their contents, hoping something useful would jump out at them.

'Look! With this spell you can become invisible.' Naz handed a book to Rachaya. 'We could sneak down to the village anytime we want with a spell like that.'

'It won't help Zeb fly, though,' said Rachaya. She waited until Naz was distracted by another book, then quickly wrote the spell down in her notebook. Every time she found an interesting spell she wrote it down to try it out later. She was writing down a spell for making objects disappear when Naz called her over.

'This could be it,' Naz said. 'It's a spell to make objects hover.'

Rachaya came over and read over her friend's shoulder.

'I don't know, it'd be better if Zeb can fly by himself,' Rachaya said. Naz's face dropped. 'But you know what, for now it could work.'

CHAPTER 16

RAMPAGING OKA

Rachaya paused outside her first Recreation session, her heart sinking. He may not have spoken to her often, but she would recognise Hektor's whiny voice anywhere. He had also signed up for Oka Handling. So had the earth dragons, Carswell and Drakan, although with Aodfin there they didn't bother Rachaya and her friends. Unfortunately, there was nothing to prevent Hektor from being as vile and malicious as he could whenever the teacher's back was turned.

Oka Handling took place in the stables. Piles of bird dung clung to the stable floors, feathers poking out of them in a fuzzy array of colour. The stench was so bad Rachaya and her friends had to cover their noses with the sleeves of their jackets. Hektor had his nose covered, too, only he was holding a handkerchief made of the finest silk. He was dressed in the most expensive clothing, his outfit would have been better suited to a dinner party than Recreation. The young lord glared over the top of his handkerchief at Rachaya.

The stable master, Mr Beacon, came out to greet them. He seemed oblivious to the tension in the room as well as the noxious smell. Mr Beacon was an elderly, squat fire dragon with crisp white hair and a long, drooping moustache.

'Yer firs' job is teh clean out yer oka's stall. They need a clean bed like, so's they can be 'appy an' 'ealthy.'

Hektor let out a noise of disgust. 'I'm not here to shovel oka dung. That's what our school fees pay you for,' he said.

'If yeh wan' to learn oka handlin' then yeh'll learn teh look after yer oka prop'ly. If yer not willin' teh do tha' yeh can shove off, yer school fees an' all.'

Rachaya covered her mouth to hide her smile. She had a feeling she was going to like Mr Beacon.

She walked along the stalls to find her oka. Each oka she passed was of a different hue and sheen to the next. There were blues, yellows, oranges, reds, pinks, purples, creams and greens. Some had glistening, shiny feathers, others were dull and fuzzy. Nyssa saw Rachaya before Rachaya saw her, and the oka let out a hoot of excitement. She rushed over to the bird's stall and gave the stupid creature a big hug. Nyssa kept rubbing her head on Rachaya's shoulder. Morhol and Naz joined her, bringing with them shovels and a wheelbarrow. Rachaya picked up a shovel and tried to clean the stall with the others, but Nyssa kept getting in the way. She nearly nicked the bird with her shovel twice. She gave up and took Nyssa with her to collect some straw so that the others could finish cleaning the stall without Nyssa's special brand of affection. Once the stall was clean and lined with fresh straw she placed Nyssa back in the stall and locked her in.

'Sorry about her,' she told her friends, embarrassed that she hadn't done as much cleaning as the others. Hektor, who was leaning against the wall with a shovel in his hand but doing little else, had been watching the whole thing.

'I hope you two are not always going to let the *princess* make you do all the work? I always suspected she was a lazy waste of space.'

'I only see one lazy person here, Hektor, and it's not Rachaya,' Naz retorted.

Hektor fumed. 'You'll pay for that remark. You'll see. Who are you to talk to your prince that way?' he asked menacingly.

Morhol took a step forward. 'Has no-one told you, Hektor?' he said with a leering smile. 'You're not our prince anymore. You're just one of many unimportant lords. Our loyalty is to our princess, and you had best remember that.'

'Or you'll do what, you filthy street rat?' Hektor said, also taking a step forward. Hektor sized up Morhol. Hektor was older, bigger and stronger. He walked up and pushed his face up close to Morhol's. 'Say just one more word to me, commoner scum, and I will flatten you to the dirt.'

'*One. More. Word*,' said Morhol. With the speed of lightning he shoved Hektor and pounced on him. Hektor may have been bigger, but Morhol was faster. He pummelled the young lord furiously. Clearly having a strong nose for trouble, Aodfin ran over to the fight. As quick as a flash, he pulled the two boys off each other and held them at arm's length.

'What do you two think you're doing?' he growled quietly. 'You're lucky Mr Beacon is calming a rampaging oka right now or you would both be in big trouble. The punishment for fighting is always detention, if not expulsion. Do you really want that?'

'A rampaging oka?' Naz said. 'There's no such thing.'

'There is when I rile one of them up to create a diversion.' His small smile betrayed a sense of humour. 'Now stop being stupid, both of you, before all of us end up in trouble.'

'What's it to you?' sneered Hektor. 'You may be Ardhan's son, but you're nothing to me.'

'No, I'm more than you,' said Aodfin, looking at Hektor as if he were a worm. 'And I'm loyal to my princess. Just you remember that the next time you think about causing trouble, *my lord*.' He shoved Hektor away from him. Hektor fell into the oka dung with a squelch and slid across the feather-caked ground for several paces. His finely tailored bottom was coated in white goop and feathers by the time he stopped. Hektor stood and stalked away, feathers bouncing merrily along with each step. Aodfin joined in the laughter with the other three.

'If he causes you any more trouble, Princess, you come to me, okay?' he said, before rejoining his friends.

'Wow,' breathed Naz when Aodfin was out of earshot. 'He sure packs a punch, doesn't he? Talk about strong. And you know what else, Chia? That's two boys in a very short space of time that have declared their loyalty for you. How do you make all the boys fall on their knees for you?' She batted her eyelashes up at Rachaya. 'I'd love to know your secret.'

Both Morhol and Rachaya became very embarrassed, and not much more was said between them as they finished cleaning up the area around Nyssa's stall. They finished their tasks early, so Mr Beacon let them leave well before the end of Recreation.

'Go tidy yerselves up a bit,' he said. 'Yeh don' want to be eatin' yer dinner covered in poop, I can tell yeh tha'!'

Rachaya and her friends rushed up to their dorms for a shower and a change of clothes. Rachaya washed the dung off as quickly as she could so she could make the most out of having an empty dormitory. Every spare moment she had recently was spent secretly practising the hover spell Naz had discovered in the library. At first she could only raise a pencil into the air. However, as she practised over the following weeks she found she could lift heavier and heavier objects. In the meantime she, Morhol and Naz continued to search for a better spell to help Zeb. Rachaya kept adding spells to her notebook and tried to teach them to herself whenever she had some spare time. Sitting on the floor in front of her bed she consulted that notebook now, refreshing her memory on how to perform the hover spell.

Rolling up her sleeves, she held her hands out in front of her. She focused on her bed, feeling the familiar warmth as magic oozed down her arms and nestled into her fingertips.

'Hover,' she whispered. The bed started to vibrate. Faster and faster it buzzed until it was rocking from side to side. It began to rise into the air until it was floating just above the floor. Rachaya found it difficult to keep the bed still, and it continued to rock until she lost control and it came crashing back to the floor. She ran over to the bed to make sure she hadn't damaged anything. The bed was empty, a fur-covered indent in the place where Tibbles usually slept. She searched the dorm from top to bottom, but her cat was nowhere to be found. Her dorm mates soon arrived from their own Recreation sessions and kindly offered to help her look for Tibbles. When the bell sounded for dinner she was forced to abandon her search. She and Naz told Zeb and Morhol about the missing cat while they ate, and her friends offered to help her search for Tibbles after Study that night.

'It's just not like her at all,' she said once again.

'Maybe she went to catch some mice?' Naz suggested.

'No, she's too lazy for that.'

After Study, Rachaya, Morhol, Naz and Zeb searched the school grounds until it became too dark for them to see clearly. They went back inside and Rachaya sat anxiously in the Level 1 student lounge with her friends. She was so worried she couldn't keep up with the conversation, and even Naz showing her a new way to ignite a sugar cube couldn't distract her. She went to bed early, leaving behind shrieks of laughter as the sugar cube blazed cheerfully away.

Going to her dorm was a big mistake. Seeing the empty spot on the bed where Tibbles normally slept made Rachaya worry more than ever. She paced the room restlessly.

Students were not allowed out of the dorm after hours, but Rachaya could not worry about a small thing like rules when her beloved cat had disappeared. Grabbing a jacket, Rachaya headed out of the dorm without a second thought. She snuck along the corridors, keeping to the shadows as much as possible. Thankfully, the Level 1 students were on the first floor so it was surprisingly easy to leave the building unnoticed. Once outside, Rachaya began to curse her thoughtlessness. It was so dark outside she couldn't see anything, only grim, looming shadows that set her heart racing. She was about to head back inside when she was struck by a brilliant idea. If Naz could ignite a sugar cube, surely Rachaya could do the same with a bunch of sticks? If she could create a makeshift torch she would be able to see well enough to continue her search.

Rachaya fumbled through the dark and made her way to the quadrangle – a small seating area that was surrounded by a grove of trees. She scrambled about on the ground to collect a handful of twigs, banging her knee on the edge of a bench and stifling her cry so no-one would hear her. Rachaya wove the sticks together using the same technique she had used to bind the fibres of bamboo in Magical Education. Then, concentrating with all her might, she directed a small amount of her inner fire onto the woven bundle of sticks. It was surprisingly easy. But now Rachaya was struck with a second problem. Light would make it easier for her to see, but it would also make it easier for a teacher to spot that she was outside after curfew. Rachaya wracked her brain and remembered a spell she had discovered during her research – the sight shield Rachaya had been practising at her desk during Study when she was bored. So far she had been able to turn her entire hand invisible. She placed the sight shield over her hand, and then extended it so that it also covered the light.

Rachaya grew frustrated. Now she couldn't see the light either. She threw down the torch. Once it was outside of her shield she could see it again. Furrowing her eyebrows, Rachaya extended her sight shield further. Out and out it crept until the torch was once again invisible. Rachaya threw out the shield like a blanket, engulfing herself and the air around her in invisibility. She picked the torch back up and rekindled it. Trusting that she had placed the shield correctly she fastened it in place, weaving it to her body in much the same way as she had woven the sticks. Rachaya was trusting her instincts and hoped that she was performing the magic correctly.

Using the lost and found spell she had learnt in Practical Magic, Rachaya attempted to try to locate Tibbles. She didn't think the spell could work on living creatures, but she had some fur on her clothing. She tried to locate that instead. She could sense some fur back in the dormitory, and also near the dining hall, but the link wasn't strong enough to suggest that Tibbles had been there recently. Not ready to give up, Rachaya cast the spell a second time. This time she felt the faintest stirring in the school orchard. Why would Tibbles have gone on a trip to the orchard? She had never been there before. Rachaya decided that this would be the best place to begin looking and surged up there as quick as her legs could carry her. Here there were trees of cherry, apple, lemon, lime, orange, mandarin, peach, nectarine, and goodness knows what else, all allowed to spread wildly so that the once neat rows now more closely resembled a forest than an orchard. By day Rachaya loved roaming the orchard on her oka, but by night it seemed creepy. The trees creaked as they swayed in the gentle breeze, setting Rachaya's already frayed nerves on edge.

Using the thought of Tibbles to fortify her courage, Rachaya entered the gloom that only trees can make. She held her light up high and extended her shield, spreading a warm pool of light to disperse the shadows. Rachaya threaded her way through the trees, ducking under branches and dodging stray roots. It was hard going, and she was puffing and panting by the time she had made it to the centre of the orchard. She paused to catch her breath. All about her was quiet; the rustling of trees was the only sound she could hear, except for her own breathing.

A meowing called out from somewhere to her right. She spun in the direction of the sound and listened. She heard it a second time, louder and more desperate. Without thinking about any possible danger, Rachaya crashed through the trees in the direction of the meow. She ran and ran until she found herself standing in a small clearing. Two green orbs glittered up at Rachaya – Tibbles' eyes reflected in the firelight. She was trapped in a sturdy iron cage.

This was no accident Tibbles found herself in.

This was deliberate.

Rachaya became all too aware of how stupid it was to come here alone without telling anyone where she was. She reduced her sight shield so that it only included herself and her torch, although it was much harder to hold on to now that she was tired. Rachaya moved cautiously toward the cage, every single one of her senses on full alert. She felt as if a thousand eyes were watching her, even though she was invisible. She stopped directly in front of the cage and looked all around her for signs of movement. She could detect nothing. Turning back to Tibbles, Rachaya carefully extended the sight shield so that it covered the cage. With the added shield around the cage, she was beginning to feel the strain of using so much magic. Deciding that she didn't need to see so well now that she had Tibbles, she extinguished her torch and waited impatiently for her eyes to adjust to the dark. Rachaya picked up the cage and headed back to the school. She moved as quietly as she could, flinching at every cracking twig or snapping branch. She kept looking back over her shoulder, expecting a villain to appear out of the shadows at any moment. Once she was back in the quadrangle Rachaya released the sight shield. She hadn't forgotten Mr Thestral's warning that non-dragon magic was forbidden at Wyvolds. Besides, she was too exhausted to hold it any longer.

CHAPTER 17

FORBIDDEN LOVE

Rachaya crept back to the dormitory building with her precious burden, using the last of her magical energy to levitate it slightly so it was easier to carry. It was well into the night by now and most of the students had gone to bed. A quick glance told her that the student lounge was unoccupied, so she carried Tibbles inside and placed the cage onto a table.

A figure emerged from the shadows. She was not alone.

'Mikel!' she exclaimed when she saw the jewel-encrusted clothing glittering in the dim light. 'What are you doing at Wyvolds?'

'I came to make sure you were settling in okay. Imagine my concern when I discovered that you had disappeared.'

Rachaya's stomach gave a funny little lurch. 'Who else knows I went missing?'

'Just your friend, Nazish, although I have half a mind to tell your Level 1 coordinator. I would have, too, if you hadn't shown up soon.' He did a double take when he noticed the cage for the first time. 'Why have you put Tibbles in a cage?' he asked in a dangerous voice.

'*I* didn't put Tibbles in anything,' she replied, angry that he would think she could be so cruel to Tibbles. 'I found her like this in the orchard. That's why I went wandering. I was looking for her.'

Mikel started to say something but stopped. He smiled, but it didn't reach his eyes. 'It seems to me like you and Tibbles are the butt of a harmless practical joke.'

'I'd hardly call it harmless. Anything could have happened to her.'

'But it didn't,' said Mikel with one of his characteristic shrugs. He reached out and, with a little wave of his hand, the lock of the cage sprang open.

'How did you do that?' she asked as she squashed Tibbles in a very big hug. Mikel showed her how to do the spell and, after a few times practising, Rachaya could perform it perfectly.

'You seem to have a knack for magic,' Mikel said thoughtfully. 'I wonder if it's the human side of you. It's a handy skill to have up your sleeve.'

'Can't every dragon do magic?'

Mikel shook his head. 'Most can do the very basic spells, but even then their magic is very weak. We usually conserve our power to aid us in transforming and flying.'

Rachaya nodded thoughtfully. 'So you think that I have a little extra magic because of my father?'

'Exactly,' replied Mikel. 'And speaking of Krishn, he's been settling into the castle brilliantly. The others have discovered his skills as a butcher so, as I predicted, he's become a firm favourite amongst the dragons there.'

Mikel asked Rachaya how she was settling in at Wyvolds, and she told him all about her friends and classes. Once he was sure Rachaya had everything she needed, including treasure to send letters to Krishn, Mikel left. He promised her he wouldn't say anything to her teachers about her night wanderings . . . this time.

'But if I catch you at it again,' he said, 'I will personally see to it that you are given a detention.'

Rachaya carried Tibbles to her dorm and was glad to find that Naz was still awake. She filled her in on the events of the night.

'I bet it was Hektor because of the fight today,' Naz said.

'No, he wouldn't have had time.'

'Then Carswell and Drakan. I'm sure they've been looking for a way to get back at you ever since Morhol punched Drakan.'

'But what if it wasn't?' Rachaya said, not convinced that a student could have had access to an iron cage to lock Tibbles up like that. 'What if it was a trap set for me that I was lucky enough to escape from?'

Naz made a rude noise. 'You're beginning to sound like Reijko. Mikel was right. I'm sure it was just a practical joke.'

Rachaya agreed, not wanting an argument, but privately she thought differently. Hugging Tibbles close, Rachaya fell into an uneasy sleep.

***

Earthsday and Sunday very quickly became Rachaya's favourite days. Not only did she have Magical Education with Miss Hobstone on those days, but she also had double Herbalism with Mr Hopp. She loved it, not least because Mr Hopp often allowed the students to leave early if they had finished all their work. Rachaya became an expert at chopping herbs at a super-fast speed so she could leave early. That way she could have spare time to practise her spells in the privacy of her empty dorm room.

Zeb kept reminding Rachaya of her promise to help him fly, so today she was extra anxious to finish her potion early. She diced and sliced and chopped faster than she ever had before. She stirred the potion feverishly until, at last, it looked and smelled just like Mr Hopp had said it should. She hastened to pour it into a beaker, slopping it everywhere, and scurried over to the teacher. The old water dragon frowned and poked at the Hypopyrexia Potion with a stirring rod.

'Hmm,' he said. 'Its consistency is a bit thinner than I usually aim for, but it will do the job. Pack up your things and you may go.'

Rachaya rushed over to her worktable and began rinsing her equipment.

'Hey, Chia, can you help me strip this white willow bark? I forgot it needs to be shredded and they need to go in next.'

Rachaya gave her friend an apologetic smile. 'Sorry, Naz,' she said. 'I really need to go practise.'

Naz shook her head and began to roughly tear apart the white willow bark herself. 'Just be careful you don't get caught,' she muttered to Rachaya out of the side of her mouth. 'Mr Thestral meant what he said about you know what being banned. He'll kick you out if he finds out.'

'No-one will find out, I promise.' Rachaya dropped the last of her Herbalism gear into her bag. She hurried from the classroom and made for her dorm. The second she entered it, however, she realised she was not going to have the privacy she would need for her magic. Lily Fisher was huddled up on her bed, sobbing as if she thought the world was going to end. Rachaya rushed over to her and placed a hand on her quivering shoulder.

'Are you okay?' she asked. Lily sobbed even louder in response.

'Do you want to talk about it?'

'It's . . . It's stupid,' said Lily, fresh tears falling down her cheeks.

'I'm sure it's not,' Rachaya said. 'You can tell me. Maybe I can help?'

Lily wiped her nose on her sleeve. 'It's Reijko,' she said. 'I'm in love with him.'

Rachaya choked back a laugh. 'You're in love with *Reijko*?' she asked. 'That's not so bad. He's quite nice.'

Lily started crying again. 'He's the nicest. That's the problem.'

'I don't understand,' Rachaya said. 'Did he turn you down?'

'How can he? He can never know.' Lily reached out and grasped Rachaya's hands. 'Chia, promise me you won't tell him.'

'Of course not,' Rachaya said. 'But, Lily, if you like him so much maybe you should tell him yourself.'

Lily's red and puffy eyes widened with fear. 'Chia,' she breathed, 'how could you possibly suggest such a thing? Don't you know it's against Wizard Law for two different dragon types to be together?'

The two girls gave a guilty start when the door to the dorm flew open. Lily's friend, Lissa, entered the room.

'Oh, Lily, you're still upset?' she asked. 'Come on, let's get you something to eat. You'll forget all about it soon enough.'

'Thanks for the chat, Chia,' Lily said as she left the room with Lissa.

Naz did a double take at Lily's tear-stained face when she walked past the water dragons into the dorm room. 'I can see it's been busy in here,' she said. 'What's wrong with Lily?' She sat down on the bed next to Rachaya. 'You aren't looking that great yourself. What's been going on? She didn't catch you, did she?'

'No, of course not,' Rachaya said. 'Can I ask you a strange question? Did you know that wizards have forbidden dragons from having relationships with other kinds of dragons?'

'Of course. Everyone knows.'

'Does it ever happen anyway?'

'Yes.'

'And the punishment?'

Naz's face darkened. 'The wizards come and take the baby away. It happened once to a neighbour of mine. She never saw her child again.'

Rachaya's stomach gurgled uncomfortably. 'That's awful!'

'Chia, how many times do I have to tell you? The *wizards* are awful.' Naz leant forward so she could look Rachaya in the face. 'Why is this upsetting you so much? You don't have a crush on Zeb or anything, do you? You guys have been spending a lot of time alone together lately.'

'Zeb? No! It's just – what if that's the reason Head Wizard Mathonwy tried to have me executed. Maybe I was supposed to be killed as a baby?'

Naz shrugged. 'It's possible, although I've never heard of the law mentioning humans at all. Why would it when we're not supposed to leave the island?' Naz grinned. 'So you don't have a crush on Zeb, then?'

Rachaya flushed crimson. 'No, I don't!'

'Good, because I don't think Morhol would like it very much if you did.'

Rachaya threw her pillow at Naz. 'You're being stupid. Come on, lunch will be ready by now.' She walked out of the room before Naz could make any further uncomfortable comments.

CHAPTER 18

RACHAYA FEELS THE PINCH

Rachaya was beginning to feel she could be a successful dragon when Mr Ruffhead made the announcement that the Level 1 students would soon be sitting examinations. The teachers started preparing the Level 1 students for their midyear exams and Rachaya started to panic – they had learnt so much in such a short space of time. How could they expect her to remember it all at once? Her friends didn't understand why she was so worried.

'I mean, it's not like you've never sat an exam before,' Naz said.

'That's the problem. I never have.'

'What, never ever?' Morhol asked. 'Even at our junior schools we had exams and tests and things.'

'Never a real exam. The teacher said there was no point to a test since we all move up a level at the end of the year anyway.'

'Humans are weird,' Morhol said with a shake of his head.

Hektor seemed to sense Rachaya's distress and did everything he could to make her feel worse. He nudged his friend as Rachaya and her friends walked past them at dinner. Hektor's friend jumped to his feet.

'Hey, have you transformed yet?' he shouted out to her. 'I'm pretty sure they don't let people move up a level until they've transformed.'

Hektor clapped his friend on the back and glared across at Rachaya, triumph shining from his face. Rachaya paled.

'Don't worry about what that idiot and his friends say,' Naz said. 'The real test is not until the end of the year. These exams are really just so that the teachers can see what areas need the most work.'

But Rachaya's real concern was not whether she passed the exams. What was truly worrying her was that she hadn't managed to transform yet, as Hektor had taken great delight in pointing out to her whenever he saw her. Everyone else in her level had managed to transform at least once. She was scared that, because she was a half-human, she would never be able to transform. What would happen to her then?

As if he could read her thoughts, Morhol offered to teach her how to transform after dinner. 'I'll be out on the landing lawn with Zeb anyway. You may as well come along and I can teach you while Zeb runs up and down trying to gain enough momentum.'

'Has he flown yet?'

'No, but he refuses to give up hope,' Morhol said.

They ate as quickly as they could and headed out to the lawn. Zeb and Morhol shouted out advice to her as she tried to will her body to transform.

'Imagine you're growing bigger!'

'Imagine your teeth are fearsome fangs!'

'Just *feel* your body transforming and it will.'

Rachaya closed her eyes and pushed with her mind forcefully until her head hurt. She gave up with a huff.

'It's no use.'

'I think your eyes have changed colour. Slightly,' Zeb said cheerfully.

'Really? You think so?'

'Yep. I'm sure you're nearly there.'

Morhol rolled his eyes. 'You are both the most optimistic dragons I have ever met,' he said. 'Come on, it's nearly Study time. We'll try again on Starsday.' He wandered off ahead of them, leaving Zeb and Rachaya on the landing lawn.

'Any luck on that flight spell yet?' Zeb asked.

'No, but I've been working on a pretty good one that can make objects hover.' Most of the students had gone inside to their dormitories to Study and the school grounds were deserted. 'Want to see?' she offered. Zeb readily agreed.

Rachaya took off her scarf and placed it on the ground. Zeb watched with a bemused expression as Rachaya extended her index finger and pointed directly at the scarf.

The magic welled up in her hand. 'Hover!' The scarf gracefully rose into the air and floated at eye level. A scarf was certainly much easier to levitate than a bed.

'Wow, that's amazing,' Zeb said, his face alight with excitement.

'Down,' commanded Rachaya, and the scarf wafted back down to the ground. She bent down to pick it up so that she could hide her satisfied smile from Zeb.

'That's so awesome, Chia. Do you think you could use that spell on me?'

'That's why I've been practising for weeks,' she said. 'I've become good enough to make my bed hover, but when you're in your dragon form you're much bigger than a bed so I'm not sure I can lift you yet. Besides, I want you to be able to do it by yourself, so I'm still looking for a better spell.'

'But flying's *flying*, even if you need help to do it,' Zeb said. 'I can't wait until you can try the spell on me. How soon do you think you can manage it?'

Rachaya thought about it for a bit. 'Maybe we can try it out now, while you're in your human form. Just once up and back down to the ground. What do you think?'

A radiant smile broke out across Zeb's square face. 'That would be incredible! What do you need me to do?'

Rachaya instructed Zeb to stand in front of her, his hands hanging loose at his sides.

'Now just relax and try not to move,' she said. 'I've never levitated anything that was moving before, and I'm not sure what will happen.' Zeb nodded, but refused to let Rachaya's warning dampen his enthusiasm.

'I won't move. Promise.'

Slowly she raised her hand, extending her index finger so it was pointing at Zeb's round belly, hoping that this was his centre of balance. If she placed the spell on the wrong spot Zeb would flip upside down in the air, although she was not going to tell Zeb that. Feeling her power well up in her finger, Rachaya shouted. 'Hover!'

Slowly, very slowly, Zeb began to move. Up he went until he was standing on the tips of his toes. He continued to rise, and next his feet were completely off the ground. Soon you could have passed a hand under him. Rachaya held him steady, not letting him float any higher.

'You did it, Chia!' he cried. 'You made me fly!'

'Don't move,' she warned him through gritted teeth, feeling her control over the magic begin to slip. Carefully she lowered him back to the ground. Her brow was slick with sweat, and she felt tired right down to her bones.

'I definitely need to keep practising,' she wheezed.

'Are you serious? That was the most brilliant, amazing thing ever. I can't wait to tell Morhol and Reijko,' said Zeb.

'Please don't tell anyone yet. I . . . I'd be embarrassed. I don't have the spell completely right yet.'

'Okay,' Zeb agreed reluctantly. 'But just imagine the look on those earth boys' faces when we fly around in front of them. Can we still keep practising this spell together if we do it in secret?'

'Yes, just as long as I can manage to catch my breath back,' Rachaya said, still panting.

Mrs Byrne came hurrying across the landing lawn, her hair flying all about her face. She spotted Rachaya and Zeb as she passed.

'Come now, Rachelle and Arkyn, it's Study time. Off you pop,' she said as she scurried past to her office. Rachaya and Zeb headed back to the dormitory building to Study, though Mrs Byrne didn't even look back over her shoulder to make sure they had obeyed her. Rachaya left Zeb and made her way across to her dormitory. She apologised for being late to the Level 5 student who was supervising.

'Just go sit down,' said the earth dragon, before going back to her book.

Rachaya sat down at her desk and pulled out her Transformation text book. She looked at the half-formed dragon on the front cover with despair. Even if her eyes had changed colour slightly, it wasn't enough to make a real dragon out of her. It also wouldn't be enough to help her pass her exam. Rachaya studied well into the night, taking her books into the student lounge once everyone else had gone to bed.

The following morning Zeb extracted a promise from Rachaya that she would help him levitate again, so that afternoon Rachaya went back down to the landing lawn with him. No-one else was outside. Exams were beginning to feel very close and most students were taking every opportunity to revise. They stood together on the grass, the only sound the clip-clipping of the gardener's shears.

'Now don't move a muscle this time,' said Rachaya. 'It makes my control over the magic slip.'

'I won't, Chia, I promise,' said Zeb. 'I won't do anything that might make you stop levitating me.'

As if in anticipation, the magic began to course through Rachaya's arm, even though she hadn't tried to summon it yet. She pointed her index finger at Zeb, who immediately stood still.

'Hover,' she said. Once again Zeb rose gracefully up into the air. He kept himself perfectly still, his only muscle movement his smile, which grew wider and wider with every passing moment. But then his smile faded and his eyes widened with fear.

'Chia, look out behind you!' he cried.

Rachaya swung around, dragging Zeb through the air with the motion. The gardener, his face covered with a hood, stood before her, his shears held aloft as if he meant to strike her. Rachaya raised her hands in self-defence, accidentally releasing her hold over the hover spell. Zeb plummeted to the ground, landing with an 'oomph' on top of her. Both students scrambled to their feet, winded and bruised. The gardener was nowhere to be seen.

'We need to get inside, right now,' Rachaya said.

They hobbled across to the dormitory building, both sore after falling so hard on the ground.

'What did that gardener mean by scaring you like that?' said Zeb. 'And then to just run off without making sure we were okay?'

Rachaya tried to laugh it off. 'He was probably just coming over to tell me off for using magic. Non-dragon magic use is against school rules. He probably went to tell Mr Thestral what I did.'

They found Morhol and Naz silently poring over their books in the student lounge. Zeb told them what had happened in an urgent whisper. Naz looked grim.

'You say his face was covered? This could be serious, Chia,' she said. 'I know I laughed about it at the time, but what if Reijko's prediction was correct? What if he was trying to hurt you?'

'What prediction?' asked Morhol and Zeb in unison.

'Reijko had a dream about me at the beginning of the year, and his augury teacher said it was a sign that I'm in danger or something.' Rachaya's heart sank.

'That's ridiculous,' Zeb said. 'Who would want to harm a thirteen-year-old girl?'

'Lots of people,' said Morhol. 'Her cousin for one, who she booted from the throne. The wizards, who she bested at the council when she came to Fyrebyrne, or so the rumours say, or even all of those dragons who have been saying that a half-human cannot possibly inherit the throne.'

Rachaya felt as if the walls were closing in on her, and her vision dimmed for a moment. 'People have been saying those things about me?'

'Yes, but that doesn't matter. We told you people would gossip.'

Rachaya felt herself becoming hysterical. 'Well there's no point worrying about it,' she said, speaking with a much more high-pitched voice than usual. 'Obviously I can't go to an adult because we can't prove that anything happened. I just need to keep my head down and pass these exams.'

'You don't have to try to be brave for us, Chia,' Naz said gently.

'I'm not trying to be brave. But I don't have any other choice. Now can we please stop talking about it before I explode?'

Naz and Morhol picked up their books and went back to studying in silence. Rachaya ignored the worried looks they kept sending her way and tried to memorise the five healing properties of the Melissa herb.

＊

Later that night Rachaya wrote a letter to her father, telling him she loved him. Her pen paused, poised above the page as she stopped in indecision about whether she should mention the gardener's attack on her. A blob of ink dropped on the page, jolting her out of her reverie. She blotted the paper clean and wrote instead about how well she was going in Oka Handling.

Mrs Vulcan, with the winged glasses and sour expression, was manning the desk when Rachaya went to the main office building to post her letter.

'Students are not allowed to post letters this late at night,' she barked.

'Please,' Rachaya said. 'I'll pay you double!'

The dragon turned purple in the face. 'How dare . . . a bribe . . . the nerve . . . get out!' the angry creature stuttered. Rachaya turned on her heel and ran back to the dormitory building.

'You went out alone?' Naz said. 'Haven't you learnt anything from this afternoon?'

'I just needed to tell my father I love him,' she choked.

Naz's expression softened and she pulled Rachaya into a hug. 'It'll be alright, Chia. We're all here to look after you. I'll even speak with Aodfin if you like, so he can look out for you, too. And I'll post your letter for you tomorrow so you don't have to face Mrs Vulcan again.'

'Thanks, Naz, you're the best.' Rachaya hugged her back. 'I might just go to bed so this day's completely over with. Tomorrow surely can't be any worse than today has been.'

'That's the spirit.' Naz sent Rachaya on her way with a friendly slog to her arm. Naz's love might be tough, but at least the pain in her arm took her mind off her worries.

CHAPTER 19

A DRAGON IS BORN

Exams hit the Wyvold the Fierce School for Dragons with full force, leaving Rachaya with no time to worry about catnappers or the attack on her and Zeb. To her surprise, Rachaya thought she did quite well on all her written exams. She was able to remember ninety out of the one hundred uses of worms' blood, but she had to make up the other ten. All she could hope was that, if she was creative enough, her teacher wouldn't notice that they weren't all correct. She was pretty certain that she hadn't mixed up Gottingern the Great with Gottvig the Cunning, even though she had always confused the two of them when she was studying.

It was the practical aspect to the examinations that Rachaya struggled with. She was so nervous in Herbalism that she used fennel instead of poison hemlock, making a potion that probably tasted nice but did absolutely nothing to cure acne. In Hopology she accidentally ducked when she should have dived and nearly caught a blow to the head. Thankfully, she was able to earn back some marks by disarming her opponent.

Thanks to all the time she had spent practising spells in secret, Rachaya managed to find the Magical Education examination easy, earning her one of Miss Hobstone's special smiles. Unfortunately Gemology hadn't been as easy, and Rachaya hadn't been able to tell the difference between blue topaz and sapphire. She thought it was a bad sign when Miss Upton huffed angrily as she wrote down Rachaya's mark in her book, although the old teacher could have just been annoyed that the exam was interrupting her nap time. Besides, as she told Naz later, she might have had more of a chance in her exam if Miss Upton hadn't spent all their lessons fast asleep.

Rachaya managed to meditate in her Personal Development exam without giggling, although Mrs Byrne didn't seem to notice, and Rachaya was almost certain the teacher had written her result under the wrong name. To her embarrassment she panicked during her Fire Studies exam when the fire she was supposed to be extinguishing blazed completely out of control. In the end Mr Cole had to put the fire out for her, and he didn't seem prepared to be lenient with her.

'It seems you are better at creating fire than you are at controlling it,' he said with a shake of his head. 'Pity, pity.' Rachaya tried not to let it bother her, even though she was certain Mr Cole didn't like her.

When Rachaya weighed up the good results with the bad she felt that perhaps she may have passed overall. But she still had Transformation, her worst subject. It was with great trepidation that she walked out to the landing lawn and stood in front of an expectant Mrs Stacey. The kindly teacher smiled up at her reassuringly.

'Just take your time, my dear,' she said softly.

Rachaya nodded and closed her eyes, which were hot with tears because of her nerves. Rachaya took a deep breath, trying her best to focus.

And then she felt it.

Deep down in the pit of her belly something seemed to shift. She became tingly all over with excitement. Rachaya opened her eyes and looked down at the ground. It seemed to be further away than usual, and it dawned on her that it was further away because she was *growing*. Up and up and up she grew until Mrs Stacey looked like she was as small as a mouse. Her spine grew longer and longer, extending out beyond her bottom and forming a sinuous tail. She could feel her teeth growing. They felt itchy. She tried to use her tongue to scratch at them, and a sharp sting told her that her teeth were now razor-sharp fangs. She could taste hot blood pooling in her mouth but her lips wouldn't work anymore for her to spit it out. Her skin was itchy, too, but when she rubbed at it, it was as hard as steel.

'Well done, Chia! You did it!' Mrs Stacey cried from far down on the ground. 'Now, see if you can change back.'

Rachaya nodded. 'Okay,' she growled, shooting sparks out of her mouth. Mrs Stacey battered away a spark that had caught on her clothing as if it were nothing more than a fly. Rachaya closed her eyes again and found it easier to flip the switch inside her that would turn her back to her human form. Down and down she shrank. She suddenly felt soft and weak and fragile. It did not take long until she was back to her human self.

'Red, just like your mother, although not quite as bright, I think. Yellow eyes too, and scarlet fire. Very similar to Adara. I thought you might be. You look so much like her when she was your age.'

'You knew my mother?' Rachaya asked.

'Yes, I taught her here at Wyvolds,' Mrs Stacey said with an odd smile. 'I had always thought it strange when she disappeared like that. But now we all know where she went. Now,' she said with a clap of her hands that made Rachaya jump, 'let me see. Faultless transformation. No hesitation when instructed to change back. I believe that makes it full marks for you.'

Rachaya couldn't stop smiling as she entered the Level 1 student lounge in search of her friends.

'You did it!' Naz cried as soon as she saw the look on Rachaya's face. 'I knew you had it in you!'

'And it gets better,' Morhol said, more excited than Rachaya had ever seen him before. 'It was just announced. There is to be a celebration feast in honour of Remembrance Day.'

'Of what?'

'You know, Remembrance Day. The anniversary of the day your great, great, great-grandfather or something signed the treaty with the wizards.' Morhol looked off into the distance with a dreamy look on his face. 'I've heard that the feasts are amazing. The tastiest food ever. They only have them if the school chancellor can be bothered coming, so I thought I'd miss out.'

'Last year's was good,' Naz said. 'But there's a new school chancellor this year. His name's Myth or something. I'm sure the school will put on the feast of feasts to impress him.'

'Do you mean Math?' Rachaya asked.

'Yeah, that's the one. How did you know that?'

'He was at my trial before I came here,' Rachaya explained. 'I think he's alright. He seemed better than the others anyway.'

'Are you serious? No wizard is okay, Chia. Are you hearing this, Morhol? Morhol?'

Naz poked Morhol in the ribs, but his mind was too far away, imagining what sort of food would be served at the feast. He spent the rest of the day happily listing all the food he hoped would be there. Rachaya became bored by about the 300th cheese platter suggestion and decided to go and write her father a letter about her exams instead. She was so glad she could finally tell him she had transformed. Her letter took far longer to write than it usually would have because Naz kept stopping her every time she thought of an exam question she may have got wrong.

When she was happy with her letter, the two girls walked across to the main office building to post it. Rachaya was glad that Naz was with her when she saw it was Mrs Vulcan manning the student help desk again.

'It's a Moonsday! I have better things to do than process your letters.' Mrs Vulcan glared angrily at them through her wing-tipped glasses. 'Come back when I'm not so busy.'

'Here, dears,' said the bucktoothed Mrs Rivulet, coming up to the window. 'I'm not so busy as Mrs Vulcan. I can process your letter.'

'Thank you,' said Rachaya. Mrs Vulcan tutted and stalked away. As Rachaya handed Mrs Rivulet the treasure for the postage fee, Mr Thestral came shuffling out of his office, looking as much like a turtle as ever. Rachaya instantly recognised the tall, bearded man with Mr Thestral as Wizard Math.

'Ah, Miss Perfero,' Mr Thestral said when he saw the two girls. 'Sending a letter, are we?'

'Yes, sir,' she said. Rachaya turned and thanked Mrs Rivulet again for her help. She and Naz then made to leave, but were stopped by Wizard Math.

'It's good to see you again, Princess,' he said. He examined her closely with his blue-grey eyes, making Rachaya feel rather awkward.

'Hello, Wizard Math,' she said when it became clear he was waiting for a response from her. 'Are you here for the feast?'

'Yes, I am. It's good to see you looking so well. Mr Thestral was just saying that you have managed to transform. But don't let me keep you.' He held the door open for Rachaya and Naz and the two girls scurried out. Rachaya made eye contact with the wizard as she left and felt a jolt of magic sizzle between them. Math frowned with confusion, but gave no other sign that he felt a thing.

Naz pointed out students who were beginning to file into the dining hall, and they hurried to join them. As they entered the lofty room they spotted Morhol, who had saved them some seats. Zeb was with Morhol, and the two boys were happily guessing what food would be served. Reijko sat next to them, clearly bored by the conversation. Aodfin came over and immediately joined the boys in their chatter.

'Honestly, you'd think they'd never eaten food before,' Naz said, rolling her eyes.

The rest of the school soon filed into the hall, and many of the students began whispering about the new school chancellor.

'He's so handsome,' said a giggly Level 4 student to her blushing friend. 'Much better looking than that awful Wizard Og.'

'That wouldn't be hard.'

'He seems so stern,' a Level 2 boy said.

'I know,' said his friend, 'I wouldn't want to cross him, that's for sure.'

'They say he's very powerful.'

'They say he's here because he did something bad.'

'No, I heard he's here because he annoyed his father, Head Wizard Mathonwy.'

Rachaya looked over to where Math was sitting with Mr Thestral and some of the higher-ranking teachers. He did seem very young compared with the other wizards who had been at her court hearing, but she didn't think he looked stern, just thoughtful.

Mr Thestral called for quiet. The students stopped mid-conversation as his nasally voice rang out across the room.

'We come here today in recognition of the great service once rendered to us by the wizards. We come in a spirit of remembrance and gratitude. We are very lucky to have joining us today School Chancellor

Math. I am sure you will all join me in welcoming him to the Wyvold the Fierce School for Dragons.'

A smattering of applause echoed out across the room. It seemed that no-one was overly thankful for the presence of a wizard. The applause stopped abruptly and Mr Thestral continued.

'On this day, in the year 734, the wizards saved us from a terrible fate. We call this the Year of Sorrow, out of respect for the dreadful loss of lives we suffered at the hands of our enemies. Today, we continue a proud and strong race, and we hold this celebration feast to commemorate our illustrious rulers, the Perfero family, as well as the Wizard Assembly, who aided them so selflessly. Let us all raise our glasses in a toast.'

Rachaya scrambled to raise her glass of water. The rest of the students did the same.

'I endure,' said Mr Thestral.

'I endure,' the students repeated. Mr Thestral raised his glass to his lips, and Rachaya copied him. As she drank from her glass, Wizard Math caught her eye and raised his glass to her before taking a sip.

'And now let us eat,' said the principal. At his word the food started to arrive, hiding Rachaya's confusion at being singled out by the wizard. Plate after plate of different types of food were brought out. Pies, pastries, roasts, stews, curries, steaming vegetables, crisp salads, breads, dips, sauces and spreads. The school had hired brownies to serve the food, small, pixie-like creatures who, Naz whispered to Rachaya, looked after home and hearth. There was enough food for even Morhol's voracious appetite.

Once she had eaten so much food she felt she would burst, Rachaya sat back in her seat and allowed the stress of exams to wash away from her. A shadow fell across her as she reclined in her chair. Rachaya turned around to find a furious Hektor standing right behind her, a murderous expression on his face.

'You're so smug, aren't you?' he hissed. 'Sucking up to Wizard Math like that. Don't think I didn't see you talking to him today. One day soon you will pay and return to me what is rightfully mine. I don't care who your mother was. You're a dirty, filthy human and you *will* pay.'

He turned on his heel and stalked off before anyone even realised he had been there. Rachaya suddenly felt ill and wanted to be alone. She made her excuses to Naz and the others and headed off to the girls' bathroom. Even in the bathroom she felt as closed in as she had in the dining hall. She made certain nobody else was about before she threw a sight shield around herself and then headed out into the school grounds. The night air felt cool and refreshing after the stuffiness of the dining hall. She went into the quadrangle and sat on one of the benches. Hidden by the trees, she released her sight shield.

'A handy trick,' came a rich, baritone voice from the shadows. 'And one I'm sure you didn't learn to do at this school.' Wizard Math stepped out of the shadows.

'You followed me?' she asked angrily.

'I wanted to make sure you were okay. Your cousin didn't look like he was being very friendly to you just now.'

'Not my cousin,' she muttered.

'But your family none the less. Is he always like that?'

Rachaya shrugged but said nothing.

'Who else knows you can form a full – and, might I add, impressive – sight shield?'

'No-one.'

'Good. Keep it that way. And Princess? Please promise me you will be careful. There are more people out there than just your cousin who have a disliking of you.'

Rachaya's heart skipped a beat. 'You think there are people who wish to hurt me?' she said, thinking of the incident with Zeb on the lawn.

'Yes,' Math said simply.

Rachaya couldn't hide her surprise at his honesty. 'Why are you telling me this?'

'Because I am a firm believer in always doing what is right, no matter how uncomfortable that may make me. Unfortunately, not everyone shares my scruples.'

'And how can I be careful if I don't know who I can trust?' she asked, voicing the concern that had been plaguing her for weeks.

'You can trust your friends, I believe. Other than that, I'm not sure yet. Those whom you can place your faith in will show themselves in time. For now, just be cautious and think through all of your actions very carefully.'

'I had a friend tell me that once before,' Rachaya said, thinking of Reijko.

'Then your friend is very wise. And might I also suggest that you learn how to better defend yourself? I hear your school has a Hopology Club you could join.'

Rachaya nodded.

'Now, you had best get back inside before anyone else notices you have gone missing,' Math said gently. He extended his hand, and Rachaya shook it. 'A bargain sealed,' he said. 'To your safety.'

Wizard Math guided her back up to the dining hall and left her in the doorway. She went back to her friends and tried to rejoin the conversation but, really, all she wanted to do was find a place where she could be alone with her thoughts.

CHAPTER 20

HOPOLOGY CLUB

Rachaya told her friends about her encounter with Math, and even Naz agreed that his advice was worth listening to. Rachaya's stomach constantly felt fluttery, and her heart, hammering away in her chest, felt as if it were working overtime. Thankfully, the midyear holiday brought some pleasant distractions. The students were allowed to go down to the local village as often as they chose, so long as they were back at the school in time for dinner. Winter didn't seem to exist on Fyrebyrne Island, so Rachaya, Naz, Morhol and Zeb spent many lazy days in the village park, eating tasty pastries from the bakery. During the occasional smattering of rain they would take cover in the many shops and cafes that were dotted around the village square. But they always made sure they never went anywhere near the Wizard Shop.

Rachaya optimistically bought herself a scale-shining kit for when she began to transform more. Naz introduced them to Pyromaniacs, a store all about fire. The shop sold unique items to burn, each creating a different coloured flame. It also sold items that would self-combust if anyone went near them. Rachaya accidentally triggered one and had the fright of her life. Zeb took Rachaya into the shop, Flying Graces, where they bought a pair of flying goggles each.

Rachaya's friends agreed she should never be left alone and they each cheerfully accompanied her wherever she wanted to go. She was truly grateful to have such good friends. The tough part came when Rachaya told Naz of her intention to join the Hopology Club once school went back, so they could learn to defend themselves. Even though Naz had taken Math's warning seriously, she wasn't sure.

'You know how difficult it is for me,' Naz said. 'I don't need any more black eyes than I already get.'

'But you'll become so much better, and I can't go by myself.'

'Why can't Morhol or Zeb go with you?' Naz asked.

'Morhol needs to join the Herbalist Club because he didn't do very well in his exams, and Zeb is terrified of Mr Ruffhead.'

Naz groaned. 'Alright. But you owe me.'

The only thing stopping Rachaya from buying a fancy new sword was the fear she would get Mikel into trouble if she spent too much of his treasure. She was sure Lady Anjela would notice if she suddenly owned lots of shiny new objects, and she couldn't shake the feeling that Hektor was reporting her every move to his mother.

Once the new school term started, they approached Mr Ruffhead about swapping from Oka Handling to Hopology Club. He was happy to have them.

'Rachaya, excellent!' he said when they showed up for the first club session. 'I was hoping you would join the Hops soon. You're more than a match for any Level 2 student, even some Level 3 students on a good day.' He paused when he saw Naz. 'And you're welcome too, of course, Nazish. Although I must ask you to wear this.' He handed Naz a ridiculous-looking red, padded helmet. Naz looked as if she were about to argue, but seemed to think better of it. She rammed the helmet onto her head with a scowl.

They began with broadswords, which Rachaya wielded with ease thanks to her time in her father's butcher shop. Naz was not so lucky and struggled just to lift it off the floor. When no-one was looking, Rachaya cast a small levitation spell on Naz's sword to make it easier for her.

Once everyone had selected a sword and paired off, Mr Ruffhead demonstrated the practise exercise. The teacher took a step forward, swung out his sword, whirled to the left, ducked, then raised his sword into the block position. He made it look like an elegant dance.

'Did you all see that?' he asked the room. 'Step, swing, whirl, duck and block. Now you try.'

The room scurried into action with students stepping, swinging, whirling, ducking, blocking and crashing into each other. But, with each 'sorry' that burst forth from someone's mouth came an improvement. Before long, the students were completing a decent estimation of Mr Ruffhead's exercise. Even Naz seemed to be doing okay, although her movements were about as graceful as a swan walking on dry land.

Next, Mr Ruffhead set the students to practise the routine with a partner, who would then block and swing in turn.

'Step, swing, whirl, duck, block. Step, swing, whirl, duck, block,' Naz whispered to herself as the two girls slowly went through the motions. A pair of Level 3 students, who had obviously done this exercise before, were moving at a much more rapid pace than the two girls. Rachaya and Naz stopped to watch the two earth dragons step, swing, whirl, duck and block with such speed it looked like one fluid motion. Rachaya was completely absorbed by the beauty of the movement, when she was suddenly brought back to reality by the feel of cold steel against her throat.

'Never take your eyes from your own battle, Miss Perfero, no matter what else is going on around you,' Mr Ruffhead said with great seriousness. 'You will pair with me. Nazish, go join Rubin and Jade for the time being.' He indicated to two Level 2 students who were moving very slowly and carefully around the arena.

Mr Ruffhead pushed Rachaya much harder than Naz had done, and soon she was slick with sweat. She felt her levitation spell slipping and she released it, hoping that Naz would be okay without it for a while. She needed her full concentration to avoid receiving a blow to the head by Mr Ruffhead's lightning-fast sword. Just when she thought she could step, swing, whirl, duck and block no longer, Mr Ruffhead called time.

'Great work, Chia,' he said quietly before raising his voice for the rest of the class to hear. 'Well done, everybody. That's it for tonight. Pack up and I'll see you all next week.'

Rachaya found Naz waiting for her by the Weaponry Dome door. The two girls went outside into the darkness together. Rachaya launched into an excited recount of her training with Mr Ruffhead, but when Naz's only response was a series of short grunts, Rachaya realised that something was wrong. Naz wouldn't admit that there was a problem at first, but eventually she caved in to Rachaya's nagging.

'It's just that I'm no good, no matter how hard I try. It's no fun spending hours doing something you're rubbish at when everyone else around you is so good. And I know you did something to the sword just so I could lift it.'

'I could only lift the broadsword because my father is a butcher. I spent my childhood carrying giant goat carcasses around. And how'd you know I did something to your sword?'

'I'm not an idiot, Chia. I can tell when something becomes magically lighter. You shouldn't be doing that sort of thing, you know.'

'Why not? It helped, didn't it?'

'That's not the point. Dragons don't *do* magic. Not really. Only wizards can do magic really well,' Naz said, becoming exasperated.

Rachaya couldn't understand. 'I don't see the problem.' Rachaya shrugged her shoulders. 'I'm probably only good at magic because my dad's a human.'

'*That's* the problem, Chia, don't you see? It's not just the trouble you'd get in if you were caught. Using magic draws attention to the fact that you're different. People don't like things that are different.'

Rachaya felt a surge of anger. 'So that's what it is, is it? You're embarrassed because I'm *different*? That's just great.' She stormed off ahead of Naz.

'Wait!' her friend called. 'That's not what I meant. I just mean that you don't want to invite any further attacks.'

Rachaya stopped dead in her tracks and whirled around to face her friend. 'So now you think that I *invited* the attacks? Like I'm after the attention or something? As if I would ever be so selfish! I can't believe you would think . . . I don't want to be your friend anymore if that's what you think of me!'

'Rachaya, wait!' called Naz, but it was too late. Rachaya had thrown a sight shield around herself and had run off into the darkness. She started to head toward her favourite spot in the quadrangle but thought better of it. If Wizard Math could find her there, so could her enemies. She didn't want to put herself in danger just because she was angry. She was done with danger. Instead she headed across to the dormitory building, knowing that everyone else would have gone to dinner by now. Once in her dorm, Rachaya released her sight shield and threw herself down onto her bed. Tears burned her eyes and she blushed furiously when she thought of the way she had turned on Naz. She hadn't meant to. She was just so scared and on edge. She could feel her pulse beating in her throat and it made her feel sick. Rachaya closed her eyes and took a few deep breaths, trying to calm herself down. Feeling across her bed,

Rachaya came into contact with the furry form of a sleeping Tibbles. She grabbed the cat and pulled her tightly to her chest. She lay like that for a very long time, finally relaxing into Tibbles' warm fur. Eventually, she fell into an exhausted sleep.

***

By the time she woke up the next morning Naz was gone, so Rachaya went across to breakfast alone. She repeated an apology over and over in her head on her way down to the dining hall. She found Naz sitting at a table by herself, shovelling enormous piles of scrambled egg into her mouth.

'I'm sorry,' Rachaya said without preamble.

Naz swallowed slowly, and the noise of her gulp sounded painful. 'I didn't mean anything by it,' she said.

'I know. I'm just so tense at the moment.'

'And I'm just bitter because I'm terrible with a sword.' The two girls grinned awkwardly at one another. Rachaya was struck by an idea.

'Hey, why don't we practise together on the days I'm not helping Zeb? With the extra exercises you'll find the weight of the sword nothing in no time.' Wanting to keep the peace, Naz agreed.

Throughout the day, Rachaya and Naz were extra friendly to each other and, soon enough, their argument was completely forgotten. In double Gemology, they planned out a training regime to help Naz become stronger. They decided to start that night because Rachaya and Zeb didn't have a flying session. After classes had finished for the day, they crammed their pockets full of biscuits from the snack tray then went across the school to the Weaponry Dome. They found Mr Ruffhead in his office and explained their intentions to him. He surveyed them carefully, scratching his chin.

'Well, I see no harm in it. It will help the both of you. You can use one of the classrooms here, so long as I'm around to supervise you.' He led them to the storeroom and selected a sword for each of them. He handed Naz a wooden sword. 'As you become accustomed to the weight you can upgrade to a heavier and heavier sword,' he said. 'I usually only have earth dragons that want to train. The other elements never seem to be too interested, so most of the swords here are too heavy for most other dragons, being not so brawny and all.' He gave Naz a wink. 'But there's no reason why you can't become as strong as any of them.' He let them into one of the classrooms attached to the Weaponry Dome and watched them go through their paces. Naz did much better with the wooden practise sword. After a few minutes he left them to it, telling them to hand their swords to him when they were done. Once they were alone Naz visibly relaxed, and the two girls were able to pick up the pace of the training exercise. Naz was surprisingly nimble when she wasn't weighed down by a heavy sword and, by the end of the hour, she was able to step, swing, whirl, duck and block almost as well as Rachaya could.

'You were right,' she told Rachaya excitedly as they made their way up to dinner. 'It was just because the weapons were too heavy for me. I can really see myself getting the hang of this.' She told Morhol, Reijko and Zeb all about it over dinner and again at breakfast the next day.

'At first I kept forgetting to duck in between the whirl and the block. I think that's why I kept getting hit on the head so often. But now I'm really getting the knack of ducking.'

'That's a shame,' Morhol said, after he had heard the same story at least fifteen times. 'I was really getting used to you being black and blue all the time. How will I recognise you now?' Naz punched him on the arm. He was still rubbing at it by the time they got to their first class, Gemology. They had to be quiet because, as usual, Miss Upton wanted to take a nap, so Naz had to stop her monologue about swords. Rachaya was relieved to be spared the delights of ducking and weaving, at least for a little while.

CHAPTER 21

TASTY FLESH AND TEETH ROTTERS

Now that she had extra training with Naz, not to mention her flying lessons with Zeb, Hopology Club, and her research sessions in the library with Morhol, Rachaya was so busy that she barely had time to worry about any danger that she might be in. She was making good progress with Zeb. She could now hold him up in the air while he moved a little, but she still didn't trust herself to hold him up when he was in his dragon form. She wasn't as successful in finding a spell that Zeb could use himself. However, she was enjoying learning all the interesting and useful new spells that she came across.

Her classes were getting harder now, and Rachaya had to work hard to keep up with her studies. Dragon Studies had been fairly easy until their teacher, Mrs Watercress, had waddled into their classroom one day and announced they were going to begin learning Dragon Runes. These funny lines and dots were difficult for Rachaya to get her head around. The other students in her class had an advantage because they had grown up seeing the runes everywhere. But for Rachaya, who had never seen them before coming to Fyrebyrne Island, it was a real struggle. Morhol, with a shake of his dark head, had refused to answer Rachaya's questions. His deep frown and serious face were a good indication that he was struggling, too. Naz was in the Level 2 Dragon Studies class, so she couldn't help. Mrs Watercress was friendly and cheerful, but she wasn't terribly good at explaining things.

'Is it a soft or a hard vowel sound?' she would ask Rachaya. 'If it's hard, you'll need to add an ubriket. Do you need to add an ubriket?'

Honestly? I have no idea, Rachaya thought, but she didn't have the heart to crush the hopeful expression on Mrs Watercress' face. 'I'll add an ubriket then,' she said, hoping that was the correct answer.

At the beginning of one of the classes, Mrs Watercress bustled into the classroom, bristling with excitement. 'Don't set up your books! Don't set up your books! I've organised a field trip for us today!' she sang out at them.

'Look at that, she's wearing makeup,' Morhol said. 'And she seems to have combed her hair.'

Mrs Watercress overheard Morhol, but she didn't seem upset. 'Well, Mr Ash, one does not head into town looking like a dowdy schoolma'am. I have a reputation to uphold!' The class laughed.

'To town!' exclaimed curly-haired Lily Fisher. 'Are we going shopping, Mrs Watercress?'

'Indeed, we are not. Well, that is to say *you* are not. I may pick up a treat or two while I'm waiting for you. You lot are going to be translating the shop signs.'

The class let out a collective groan. 'Oh, don't be like that. It'll be fun,' Mrs Watercress said. 'You'll find many of the stores have a very different name in Dragon than in the Common Tongue. To this day, I still find it all absolutely fascinating.'

Mrs Watercress handed out a work sheet to each of the students. It had the Common names of several shops, spaces for the Dragon Runes, and spaces for the direct translations. Rachaya shoved the work sheet into her schoolbag and joined the rest of the class as they headed down to the village.

'You have an hour,' said Mrs Watercress. 'If any of you need me, I'll be having a bang-up meal in the pub. Now, off you go.'

Their first stop was the butcher – something Rachaya felt she should know but didn't. She stood staring blankly at the sign. She couldn't see much difference between the runes on the butcher's and the runes on the shop next door. Her mother's ring grew uncomfortably warm on her finger, distracting her from the butcher's sign. It grew so hot she had to take it off, holding it carefully in the bunched-up sleeve of her blazer. She looked around at the rest of the class and saw that they were madly scribbling on their work sheets. Rachaya darted into her bag to take out her own work sheet, causing her precious ring to fly out of her blazer cuff and fall onto the cobblestones with a clatter.

'My ring!' she cried as, before her very eyes, it rolled into an impossibly narrow gap between two cobblestones. She watched hopelessly as her classmates moved on like a flock of sheep to the next shop, none of them comprehending that she had just lost something so precious to her. Only Morhol stayed behind to help.

'Never mind,' he said sympathetically. 'We'll get it back in no time.' He crouched down to the stone Rachaya was pointing at and shoved his fingers down the crack.

'I can't quite get a grip on it,' he said through gritted teeth. 'There's nothing else for it.'

'So you're just going to leave it there?' demanded Rachaya. Morhol handed her his schoolbag and she numbly took it. He cocked an amused eyebrow at her.

'No such luck. I'll just take out the stone. It's easy enough.' Morhol expertly placed his fingers evenly along the edge of the stone and, with a small grunt, plucked it out of the ground.

'I didn't know you could pick cobblestones up like that,' Rachaya said.

'You'd be surprised what treasures people drop in them. Take this ring, for example,' he said, fishing it out of its hiding place. 'Back in the day I could have sold this in the blink of an eye. Would have fed me and my mum for a fair few weeks, I'd say. But here...' he placed the ring in Rachaya's hand and took his bag back from her. 'It belongs to my princess, so back to her hand it goes.'

'You really fed your mother by finding and selling jewellery?'

Morhol shrugged, embarrassed. 'Sure. Amongst other things.' He opened his mouth to explain further but stopped mid-sentence, his jaw hanging slack. Rachaya turned to see what he was looking at. There, coming toward them, was a hulking great figure, larger even than an earth dragon. The creature was shrouded in a dark cloak that obscured its features. It moved menacingly and Rachaya thought she saw the glint of a steel blade. Morhol placed himself in front of Rachaya, seizing the cobblestone he had prised up earlier in one fluid movement. Rachaya's hand itched for a sword. The creature drew closer and closer. Her blood pounded and her eyes burned.

A bell tinkled and the three of them turned to see Mrs Watercress step out of the village pub. Rachaya turned back. The creature had gone.

'What are you two doing? Where is the rest of the class?' asked the teacher.

'Rachaya dropped her ring and I was helping her fetch it. The others moved on,' said Morhol. Mrs Watercress seized the work sheet from Rachaya's hand. Rachaya looked up at it in dismay. It was all scrunched up. She must have been gripping it tightly in her fear.

'Miss Perfero, this is not good enough. You haven't completed even one of these exercises. Neither have you, Mr Ash. And the state of this sheet? It's just downright disrespectful. I will see the both of you in my office at lunchtime today. Now come with me. We need to find the rest of the class.'

Mrs Watercress wobbled off as fast as she could, leaving the two students no time to give any sort of an explanation. Rachaya and Morhol trundled along behind the teacher as they rejoined the rest of their class. Aodfin looked at them curiously but said nothing.

***

Naz and Zeb couldn't believe their ears when, during the recess break, Morhol told them what happened.

'Didn't you tell Mrs Watercress that you were nearly attacked?' Naz asked.

'She didn't give us a chance.'

'No, she just gave us a lunchtime detention and hurried off,' Rachaya said heavily.

'And you're sure this creature was going to hurt you?' asked Zeb.

'I'm certain of it. I even saw a knife in its hand. I think it was the same creature as before.'

'Oh, Chia!' Naz cried, pulling her into a hug. 'What are we going to do? Should we go to Mr Thestral?'

'No,' Morhol said. 'What would he do? He's just a paper pusher.'

'Mr Ruffhead, then? He likes you, Chia.'

'Yes,' said Rachaya firmly. 'I'll tell him in Hopology Club tonight. I'm sure he'll take it seriously.'

Rachaya was almost glad for the lunchtime detention because she couldn't help looking over her shoulder wherever she went. All through Herbalism she was on edge, and her friends' whispered conversation about who they thought had tried to attack them didn't help. Mrs Watercress made Rachaya and Morhol complete crisp new work sheets using their Dragon-to-Common-Tongue translators. Rachaya still struggled to see any difference between the runes, but she got there in the end. And Mrs Watercress was right, the direct translations were amusing. For example, the butcher shop translated to Pre-Cut Tasty Flesh and the sweet shop translated to Teeth-Rotter.

Unfortunately, Rachaya's bad day wasn't about to end there. As she entered the Weaponry Dome with Naz, she heard a voice that made her stomach sink.

'And so you see, sir, I really think I'd get much more out of Hopology than I would Oka Handling.'

'As long as you're willing to work hard, Mr Perfero, you are welcome to join the club,' Mr Ruffhead said to Hektor.

'What's he want to be here for?' hissed Naz.

'I don't know, but I'm sure he has nothing good in mind.'

The two girls found a weapon each and began going through the warm-up exercise. Hektor seemed content to leave them alone and they were soon able to forget that he was there.

Hektor's arrival made the number of members in the club uneven, so he trained with Mr Ruffhead. Raised a prince, Hektor had been training with weapons since before he could walk, so he was very good. Despite all the extra hours she had been training with Naz, Hektor made Rachaya look sloppy and clumsy by comparison. Hektor and Mr Ruffhead moved so fast they became a blur, and both were soon panting with the effort.

'Very good, Hektor,' Mr Ruffhead said, calling the warm-up to a halt. 'I can see you have certainly not been slacking with your practise.' Mr Ruffhead then told them to start on the drill they had been working on over the last three weeks. 'Miss Perfero, you work with me for a bit,' he called over the crash and clang of students. 'Hektor, would you mind working with Nazish for a little while?'

'Not at all,' Hektor said with a wicked gleam in his eyes.

Rachaya didn't have time to worry about Naz. Mr Ruffhead came at her with full force, and she had to work hard to keep up. 'I've been wanting to talk to you about something that happened today,' she gasped between each clash of the sword.

'Later,' grunted Mr Ruffhead, never once taking his eyes off Rachaya's gleaming sword. They stopped abruptly when, behind them, they heard the sickening sound of metal crashing into a skull. Mr Ruffhead threw down his weapon and ran over to the fallen student. Through the gap in his legs Rachaya saw a student lying crumpled in a heap on the floor. It was Naz.

'I'm so sorry.' Hektor didn't look the least bit remorseful. 'She tried to go too fast. I told her she didn't have to try to keep up with me.'

'She'll be fine,' said Mr Ruffhead, although his face had turned very pale. He picked Naz up as easily as Rachaya was able to lift Tibbles. 'All of you see to it that these weapons are packed away properly. I'll take Miss Cinder up to the hospice.'

As soon as the teacher left with the still unconscious Naz, an excited babble broke out. Hektor's voice rose above the rest.

'I did my best to make her go slower, I truly did. But she seemed to be trying to prove some sort of point. What that was, I can't even imagine.'

'It's not your fault, Hektor. Naz's known to be super clumsy. She should know by now that she's never going to be any good at Hopology.'

Rachaya couldn't get the image of her friend, lying on the floor at an unnatural angle, out of her mind. She wanted to cry, but refused to let Hektor see it. She worked together with the other students to put away the weapons, all the while biting back the tears. The rest of the club filed out in twos and threes, still discussing what had happened to Naz. Rachaya couldn't bear it a moment longer. She found a sword that had somehow escaped being packed away.

'I'll just put this in the storeroom,' she called out brightly to the others. 'Go on ahead. I'll catch up.'

She ran back to the storeroom without waiting for a response. Once inside the small, dark room Rachaya's legs gave way beneath her. She sank down to the floor and gave in to her tears. Slowly, she stopped crying. She was exhausted. Wrung out. Her breathing gradually slowed and she dried her eyes.

With a sharp intake of breath, Rachaya froze. She strained her ears. She could have sworn she had heard the shuffling of feet nearby. She waited and waited, painfully aware that she was still very much in danger. She quickly created a sight shield and left the storage cupboard. She looked around the Weaponry Dome but there was no-one else about. Cursing herself for her foolishness Rachaya dropped her sight shield and left the Weaponry Dome via the large front double doors.

'Gotcha,' she heard, before something heavy hit her on the head.

Everything went black.

CHAPTER 22

FRESH DRAGON SOUP

Rachaya woke up feeling fuzzy and warm. She touched a hand to the back of her head. It came away wet and sticky. She forced herself to concentrate. It must be blood. Did she hit her head when she fainted?

The fuzzy feeling slowly faded, leaving behind a throbbing head and the memory of a harsh voice right before something had hit her. She tried to still her rapid breathing in the hope that whoever had knocked her out hadn't realised that she was awake yet. She listened carefully. All was quiet. It seemed like she was alone. Rachaya looked around her as far as she could without moving her head. Peering through the darkness, she could see the gnarled trunks of trees, pale against the gloom of night, so she guessed she was in the orchard. The crunch of approaching footsteps interrupted her inspection, and Rachaya closed her eyes and pretended she was still unconscious. The footsteps came closer and closer. Through her eyelids, Rachaya could see that a light was being held above her face.

'Hmmm, not much to it, but I'll enjoy eating it anyway,' said a deep, stupid voice. 'Crush it. Mush it. Turn it into soup, yes, yes.'

Rachaya lay petrified with terror. She felt a hot, stinking breath blowing on her face. Knowing that meant the creature was very close to her, Rachaya kicked out as hard as she could. Her foot collided with lumpy flesh. The unexpected attack caused whatever it was to let out a yowl, and it fell over backward. Rachaya scrambled to her feet and tried to run. The creature came to its senses quickly, easily catching her with its giant, gnarled hand and she was finally able to see the creature clearly, its hideous face illuminated by the blazing fire of a torch. With thin wisps of hair clinging to the green-tinged skin of his rounded head, a squashed nose that looked like it had been broken several times and two large fangs jutting upward from his lower jaw, the beast wasn't exactly what Rachaya would describe as easy on the eyes. His body was large, squashy and ill-proportioned. His arms were far longer and bulkier than his legs, and the toes on his feet were thick and thorny. He had three fingers on each hand, all of which looked large and clumsy. By the size of him, Rachaya knew for certain that this was the cloak-draped figure that had tried to attack her on the landing lawn and in the village. Unless there was more than one of these creatures after her.

The creature sniffed her hair. 'Mmm. Fresh and tasty.'

Rachaya struggled in his grip. 'What do you want?'

'Only to eat you. I haven't had dragon meat in a long time.' The creature bared its broken brown teeth at her. 'I miss it.'

'But why me?' asked Rachaya.

A dreamy expression passed across the creature's face. 'My kind master, he says to me, "You've served me well, you have, my most faithful servant. I know how to reward you. There's a dragon, young and supple, who'll makes a goodly meal for you."

'I was surprised by his words. "I'm not allowed to eat the dragons," I say.

'My master nodded at my confusion. "Ah," he says to me, my kind, kind master. "Ah, but this one's only a *half* dragon. The other half is human, so I'm pretty sure you can eat it."'

With a swipe of its clumsy paw, the monster wiped at the drool that dripped from its thick grey lips. 'My master truly is the kindest master.' He gave a happy sigh. 'And now I've finally got you in my cooking pot he will be very happy with me.'

'He sounds wonderful,' said Rachaya sarcastically, still struggling against the creature's iron grip. 'I really must thank him some time. What's his name?'

The beast laughed. 'If you don't know then I'm not telling.'

Taking advantage of the creature's momentary distraction, Rachaya managed to lean across ever so slightly. Just enough to bite the creature, hard, on the arm.

'Yeowww,' he cried, but still he held on tight. 'Naughty dragon.' He thumped her on the head and, once again, her world turned black.

This time, when she came to, Rachaya knew exactly where she was and why. A pressure on her wrists told her that the horrible creature had taken the added precaution of tying her up. Rachaya twisted her mother's ring around her finger three times. All she could hope was that Mikel would reach her before she became the main ingredient in this creature's dragon soup.

A merry fire was crackling away beside her, a huge cauldron hanging above it. The vile beast had clearly come well prepared for his dragon feast.

Rachaya began to run through all the spells she had taught herself and how they might possibly help her until Mikel arrived. Without being able to move her hands it was going to be difficult to direct her magic, so most of her spells would be useless to her. Thinking hard, she remembered how she had been able to direct her inner fire onto a makeshift torch when she had rescued Tibbles from the orchard. She wondered if she could use the same trick to burn through the rope binding her hands. Her pounding head, twice as sore now, made it difficult to concentrate. To make matters worse, the beast was watching her closely while he tended his fire.

She desperately needed more time.

'What are you?' she asked, all the while concentrating on sending a small amount of fire magic down her arms.

'You're stupid.' He drew himself up proudly. 'I am an ogre.'

'I've never heard of ogres before,' she said truthfully.

'What do they teach you up at that school, if not about important people like ogres?'

'Oh, about flying and reading and how to be a dragon,' rattled off Rachaya, hardly aware of what she was saying. Her eyes darted about, trying to catch sight of the beast's master or any other foul ogres, all while trying to send fire magic down her arms.

'What? You lot don't already *know* how to be dragons? Us ogres, we already know how to be ogres without anyone telling us. Bah!' he spat. 'You dragons are stupid.'

Rachaya stifled a gasp as the rope started to burn. She hoped the ogre wouldn't smell the smoke. She needed to keep him distracted.

'Obviously being an ogre is easier than being a dragon if you already know all there is to it. There's just too much involved in being a dragon for anyone to know it all from birth.'

'Easier being ogres? How dare you! I'll have you know it's very complicated, being an ogre. First you need to know how to clobber.' He smacked the ground hard to demonstrate. Rachaya used the noise as an opportunity to rip the rope apart.

'Second, you need to know how to look fierce.' The ogre scowled to show Rachaya just how fierce he could be, once again displaying its crooked brown teeth.

'And third, you need to know how to make scrumpy meals. I'm especially good at that,' he said proudly. The ogre noisily smacked his lips together. 'Speaking of which, my soup must be just about ready for the fresh dragon meat.' He shuffled over to the pot with great excitement. Taking out a spoonful of liquid and blowing on it gently, the ogre tasted the soup. 'Mmm, perfect,' he said, licking his thick lips. 'Time to add the dragon meat.' He replaced the spoon and picked up the largest butcher's knife Rachaya had ever seen. He shuffled over to her, a grin splashed across his gruesome face. She panicked. Even with her hands free, there was very little she could do against such a beast. He was so much bigger than her. She knew she could never fight him off. Desperately she tried to transform, going red in the face with the effort. But in her terror, she seemed to be incapable of such a difficult feat.

'Why are you pulling faces at me?' asked the ogre. 'It won't help. You don't scare me.'

He came at her and, without thinking, she shoved the ogre as hard as she could in his barrel chest. His tunic blackened from the fire magic still gathered in her hands, and Rachaya shouted the first spell that came to mind.

'Up!' she cried, shooting magic through her fingertips to levitate him. Weightless, the ogre flew through the air and landed bum-first onto the fire. The beast bellowed with rage as his bottom sizzled, and he scrambled to get out of the flames.

The ogre's green skin turned purple with fury, and he charged at her, crashing through his carefully prepared bowl of oils and spices. Rachaya was able to smoothly dodge him, silently thanking Naz for all the hours they had spent practising Hopology. She darted to the other side of the smouldering fire pit and shot small sparks of fire at him through her fingertips. The ogre let out a roar of pain and desperately began to batter at himself as Rachaya's flames ignited the oils and spices covering his skin.

'You're not a dragon. You're a wizard! Why did master not tell me you're a wizard?'

Rachaya raised her hands to shoot more fire at him but stopped when a flaming yellow dragon swooped down at them.

'Mikel!' Rachaya shouted with triumph. She dove to the ground as the dragon, jaws wide, descended upon them.

'Aargh,' she and the ogre screamed in unison. She rolled out of the way just in time for Mikel to snap his jaws down over the ogre. With a downward thrust of his enormous wings, he launched himself back up into the sky and flew back the way he came, taking the ogre with him. Rachaya lay on the ground shaking, the reality of what had just happened taking over her entire body. She was crying, deep uncontrollable sobs, by the time Mikel returned and landed gently on the ground next to her.

'Rachaya, are you okay?' he asked urgently. He helped her sit up and pulled her into a hug. He held her while she cried out her terror and anger. He held her until she had cried herself hoarse and she felt weary to her bones.

They sat together in silence in the quiet orchard, each lost to their own thoughts, until Mikel let out a low moan, as if in pain. She pulled out of his arms and knelt beside him, placing a hand on his shoulder.

'Mikel, what's wrong?' she asked. 'Are you hurt?'

He bent over, clutching his stomach. 'I don't think I should have eaten the ogre.'

CHAPTER 23

ADARA'S WOES

The quiet was pierced by the sound of Mikel retching nearby. Eventually the noises stopped and Mikel staggered back to the clearing looking far from his usual, pristine self. His skin was pale and clammy, his hair was mussed and he had grass stains on his trousers.

'It seems that ogre meat doesn't agree with me,' he croaked. He came and sat beside her on the ground. 'How're you feeling?'

'Sore. Weak,' she said.

Mikel studied her face closely. 'It's not just that, though, is it? Rachaya, what exactly happened here tonight?'

'The ogre you ate had been trying to capture me all year. Tonight he finally succeeded.' Rachaya huffed out a sigh and had to fight the urge to cry again. 'He said that his master gave him permission to eat me because I'm only half dragon. Why would anyone do that?'

'His master? Are you sure that's what he said?'

Rachaya nodded forlornly. Mikel rubbed his hand over his face and, for the first time since she had met him, Rachaya thought that he looked his age.

'Ogres don't generally have masters,' Mikel said. 'To be honest, I always thought that they were too stupid to understand the concept of servitude, let alone follow basic commands.'

Rachaya chuckled and found that it hurt to laugh. 'So I shouldn't expect a whole bunch of ogres to come after me, wanting to roast me for their evening meal?'

Mikel put a comforting arm around her shoulders. 'Not anytime soon. I think whoever sent the ogre would be wary of trying to attack you after this. For a while, anyway.' To her surprise, tears were visible in the corners of Mikel's eyes. 'Rachaya, I have to tell you something. I hope it won't panic you,' he said shakily, once he had regained his composure. Rachaya wondered what could possibly be worse than the night she had just had.

'Many years ago, when your mother and I were young and as close as brother and sister, your mother came to me and told me that she feared she was in some sort of danger. I didn't take her seriously at first. She was the much-loved Crown Princess. I didn't think that there could possibly be a single person anywhere who didn't love her as much as I did, nor did I think anyone would want to harm so much as a hair on her head.

'To my sorrow, I was very, very wrong. Bad things started happening to Adara. Small things that could easily be dismissed as accidents. But all too soon, I could no longer write these incidents off as unhappy coincidences. One day, Adara and I were out riding our okas. She was a superior okawoman, and I am certain that is the only reason she lived that day. A hideous demon showed up out of thin air and tried to snatch Adara right off her oka's back. I charged at the demon, catching the beast by surprise, giving your mother just enough time to escape. The demon disappeared as quickly as it had arrived.' Mikel covered his face with his hands at the memory. 'Adara was in a panic. It was all too clear that someone meant to harm her, and that they wouldn't stop until she was dead. I urged her to go to the king, to ask him for extra protection. She brushed me off, telling me she would think about it. That night she went to bed early, her face pale and frightened. That face still haunts me to this day. The next morning I awoke to an uproar in the castle. The princess had disappeared sometime during the night, leaving no hint as to her whereabouts. Only I knew that she was fleeing something, and she had sworn me to secrecy.' Mikel clenched his fist.

'I was angry. She should have taken me with her. I would have given my life to protect her. I searched all over Fyrebyrne Island, and throughout Escoria. Even the Lands Beyond the Impenetrable Mist. There was no sign of her anywhere. But I never gave up hope.' He smiled grimly.

'And then I found you, giving off a magical scent remarkably like your mother's. And I found out I was too late. Adara was dead. But I was happy, too, knowing that she had been surrounded by love and acceptance at the time of her death. Surely that's a much better way to go than at the hands of some monster?' He gently placed his arm around her shoulder.

'Adara always wanted to be a mother. She would have been very proud of you. The way you handled yourself with that ogre today shows you truly have Adara's spirit.'

Rachaya realised she was crying and quickly wiped her eyes. Mikel pulled her into a hug.

'Thank you for saving me,' she said. 'How did you know where to find me?'

'The ring, of course. When we were very little your mother and I figured out that my chief adviser's ring and the heir's ring were connected to each other. Although, the ring only took me as far as Wyvolds and I had no idea where you would be once I got here. Thankfully your captor was an ogre. Only an ogre would be stupid enough to use the orchard as a hiding place twice. If you hadn't been here, I don't know where I would have looked.' Mikel was more worried than Rachaya had ever seen him. Gone were all traces of his usual cheeky grin.

'You have some very angry friends, by the way,' he said. 'Apparently you had promised them that you would make sure you were never alone.'

'I wasn't supposed to be alone, but Naz got hurt in Hopology Club. Hekt . . . someone hit her on the head and she had to be taken to the hospice.'

'Hmm, well you are going to need a better excuse than that, I think, judging by the look on young Morhol's face. Now, do you think you are able to walk? My nausea has passed so I think I am ready to brave the school.' He helped Rachaya to her feet and they hobbled back to the school together. Rachaya wanted to head straight to her friends, but Mikel stopped her.

'I'm afraid this time you can't just sneak back inside the school without anyone knowing of your little adventure. I had to notify the principal that you were missing. He will want to know you're safe.'

Rachaya nodded glumly and allowed herself to be steered into the principal's office. Only it wasn't Mr Thestral who was sitting behind the principal's desk. It was Wizard Math. And he did not look pleased.

'You have returned,' said Math, thunder in his voice. 'Prince Mikel, if you would kindly allow us a moment alone?'

Mikel nodded and bowed from the room, but not before he gave Rachaya a supportive squeeze on the arm.

'I thought I warned you not to be alone,' said Math quietly. His quiet voice was much more terrifying than yelling would have been, and lightning was flashing in his blue-grey eyes. Even his bushy black beard was trembling with barely-suppressed rage.

'My friend was hurt,' she said in a small voice. 'In Hopology Club.'

'And the rest of the club were injured, too, were they? You were the only person left standing, so there was no-one left to accompany you up to dinner?' Rachaya shook her head and looked down at her feet. Math came around the desk and gently lifted her chin with his forefinger.

'I have reason to believe that you may be in grave danger, even now. I would rather that you were kept safe. Please be more careful.'

Rachaya nodded.

'Now, tell me what happened.'

Rachaya told Math everything, glossing over her use of magic to hold the ogre off. He listened in silence. His face became more and more sombre as Rachaya's story progressed. Math sat in deep thought long after Rachaya had finished talking, dragging out the awkward silence. Rachaya shuffled her feet slightly, bringing Math back to the present.

'Well, at least you have finally learnt to keep quiet about your magic use,' he said. 'I assume that's how you managed to hold the ogre off long enough for Mikel to rescue you? I know you still find it difficult to transform.'

'Yes, sir,' she replied. 'Sir, can I ask you something?'

'Why, yes, the beard is one hundred per cent real,' he said with a twinkle in his eye.

Rachaya forced out a rough chuckle. 'No, not that, although I had wondered,' she said. 'It's just that the ogre accused me of being a wizard. Why would he think that when he knew that I was a dragon?'

Math scratched his bushy beard thoughtfully. 'I've been wondering the same thing since I saw you conjuring up a near-perfect sight shield on Remembrance Day. Dragons are magical – they have to be to fly, transform, and breathe fire. However, their magic is less tangible, less malleable than a wizard's. All I can think is that, with your mother running away from the island, and your father therefore being a human, some part of your brain has been able to tap into that which is not normally accessible to dragons. Please don't let anyone know of what you are capable of.'

'Why?'

'That's a fair question, and I know I owe you an answer after what you have been through tonight, so I'll do my best to explain. Dragons are dangerous creatures. By their very nature they are the natural leaders of the world. A dragon who can also wield magic like a wizard – that must surely seem too much of a threat to all other creatures. You already have one powerful enemy. You don't want any more.'

Rachaya nodded thoughtfully. 'But I don't know how to use magic properly, so it's not really a threat, is it?'

'Not being able to wield your power as well as you would like merely adds to your vulnerability. It will do nothing to allay the fear in others.'

'So I'll need to hide it forever and ever?'

'Yes, unless . . .' Math paused, looking uncomfortable. The look on his face was very similar to the one Zeb had every time he tried to fly, like a violent battle was raging inside his head. All of a sudden it seemed as if Math had come to a decision.

'Rachaya, how about next year I teach you how to use your magic whenever I am up at the school for my duties as chancellor? Obviously we would have to keep it a secret, even from your friends. There are many who would not look kindly upon my assisting you.'

'You would do that? Why?'

'Because I think it's about time the dragons had a strong ruler who can protect their own.'

'Even if it means training a potential threat to yourself and all the other wizards?' countered Rachaya.

Math let out a big, deep laugh. 'You're shrewd, aren't you?' he said. 'That's a good thing in a ruler. Always trust your natural instincts.

Rachaya, I believe that if you live a good life, treating all creatures with respect, others will treat you in the exact same way. I have no wish to make an enemy out of anyone. Especially not someone who could become as dangerous as you could be one day.'

Rachaya was impressed. He was being so open and honest, and it decided her. 'Alright, Wizard Math,' she said. 'I'll accept your help.'

'Just promise me one thing. Promise me you won't try to teach yourself anything that seems dangerous or complicated. Bring those things to me first.'

Rachaya agreed. Math held out his hand and Rachaya shook it, sealing the bargain. At that moment, Mr Thestral ambled into the room looking as turtle-like as ever.

'Ah, Rachaya, you have returned, I see. Prince Mikel was just telling me you fainted after seeing your friend hurt, and you became disoriented and wandered off. How do you feel now?'

'Much better, thank you, Mr Thestral.'

'Excellent, excellent. Although you do have a nasty bump coming up on your head. I recommend you go to the hospice immediately. Such things, I find, are best attended to at once, in case you have blood on the brain.'

Rachaya thanked the principal and turned to leave.

'Trust Mikel,' whispered Math as she walked past him to the door. Rachaya made no response. Mikel was waiting for her outside the office.

'How are you feeling?' he asked, concern written all over his face.

'I'm fine. Mr Thestral says I'm to go to the hospice, though.'

'Good idea. I'll walk you there. And Chia?'

'Yes?'

'What happened in the orchard tonight, please be careful who you tell. I think it's . . . best . . . if as few people as possible know.'

'Wizard Math just said the same thing to me.'

The school nurse fussed over Rachaya the second they walked through the hospice door, preventing any further conversation.

'A nasty blow to your head. You'll have to stay overnight so I can keep an eye on you,' said Mrs Rivulet in a steady stream of words. She shooed Mikel away.

'I'll come back tomorrow,' he called before the hospice door slammed shut in his face. Mrs Rivulet soon had Rachaya in a pair of pyjamas and lying in bed. She prodded and poked the princess for several minutes, tutting all the while.

'Next time you feel faint, sit straight down and put your head between your knees. Falling flat on your face is a nasty business. Unless you're an earth dragon. They always seem to grow stronger and stronger with each blow. Now you get some sleep. I'll be nearby, should you need anything.'

Mrs Rivulet finally left Rachaya alone and she studied the room. Naz was in a bed nearby, but she was fast asleep and Rachaya didn't want to bother her. Rachaya lay awake for a long while, replaying the events of the evening in her head over and over again. Eventually, exhaustion took over and she fell into a restless sleep.

When Rachaya awoke the next morning, she discovered that Mikel had organised a surprise for her. He had flown back to Perfero Castle during the night and returned with Krishn. Rachaya squealed when she saw her father.

'It's so good to see you,' she said, diving into his arms. Krishn crushed her tightly in his customary bear hug.

'I've missed you so much, Chia,' he said. 'Your letters have been great, but nothing beats seeing you here in person.' He held her out at arm's length, a serious expression suddenly on his face. 'Mikel told me what happened. Everything – warts and all. You need to look after yourself. I need you back at the end of the year. Home with me, where you belong.'

'I've organised some protection for you,' Mikel said. 'Subtle. You probably won't even notice, but it will be there. No-one except a select few know about it. But in return, you need to watch your back, okay?'

Rachaya nodded, looking at the two men who cared about her so much. She was so lucky to have as much as she did.

After she ate a tray of breakfast, Mrs Rivulet reluctantly gave her permission to leave the hospice. Rachaya spent the morning giving her father a tour of the school. She had begun to feel at home at Wyvolds and it was fantastic to be able to show her father all the places she had written about in her letters. She was even able to introduce her father to Naz, Morhol and Zeb, who anxiously ran up to her in the corridor to find out how she was.

Her friends walked back to class with her after her father had flown away from Wyvolds on Mikel's glistening yellow back. She filled them in on everything that had happened in the orchard, being careful not to mention her meeting with Math afterward.

'But ogres aren't allowed to eat dragons!' exclaimed Morhol.

'Someone told him that, because I am half-human, it would be okay.'

'Who would do something like that?' Naz asked.

'Probably another ogre,' Zeb said.

'And Mikel really *ate* the creature?' asked Morhol. 'Eww.'

'He was sick everywhere afterward.' Rachaya laughed.

'But Mikel still thinks you're in danger?' Naz asked in a low voice.

'Yes, but I have great people surrounding me, and every single one of them has my back. Mikel doesn't think anyone would try to harm me for a while, but when they do I will be ready. We will all be ready.'

NAZ AND ZEB TAKE ON WYVOLDS

A Story of The Rachaya Series

This short story takes place one year before the events of Fyrebyrne Island

CHAPTER ONE

PREPARATIONS

Naz Cinder crouched beside the sofa, praying the top of her head would not be visible to anyone entering the room. This *had* to work. It had to. She resisted the urge to peek over the arm of the chair at the sound of tentative footsteps coming from the doorway. She held her breath. Any moment now.

There! The creaking floorboard. She leapt up from her hiding position and dashed over the couch, spear tackling her little sister, Sunni, to the ground.

'Hey!' Sunni cried. 'Get off me.' She battered futilely at Naz's encircling arms.

'Tell me where you hid it,' Naz hissed, her ears alert for any sign of their mother returning home from the store, even as she struggled with Sunni's flailing arms.

'I don't know what you're talking about.' Each word was punctuated with a slam of her small fist on Naz's arm.

'Yes you do. Where's my diary, Sunni? I need to pack it into my suitcase for school.'

Sunni stopped struggling but Naz did not let her go. She knew her sister better than that.

Sunni's eyes slid to the side as if looking for a way out, but Naz had timed this with military precision. Their mother would still be out buying the last-minute supplies Naz had so cunningly forgotten to purchase yesterday just so she could have this moment today.

'*Sunni*,' Naz said, squeezing her sister's arms slightly in warning.

'I don't see why you get to go to Wyvolds and I don't.'

Naz bit back a sigh. So they were back to that old argument, were they?

'Because you are two years younger than me, and when Mum gave in to your nagging and took you to be assessed, Principal Thestral said you're not ready yet.'

Naz thought she heard her mother's distinctive wing flaps out on the street.

'Fine.' She released her sister. 'Keep the stupid thing. I'll get a new one from the village near my new school.'

She climbed to her feet and held out a hand to Sunni, but her sister refused to take it. The clever creature had heard the whump whump of their mother's wings, too. She remained on the floor, looking dishevelled, and even squeezed out a couple of tears from the corners of her eyes. Sunni knew exactly how Mrs Cinder would react to her appearance and was determined to milk the moment for all it was worth.

With a growl of frustration, Naz stalked off to the small room she shared with Sunni to finish her packing. By the end of today she would be safe in her new school, away from her annoying sister. All of a sudden Naz couldn't wait.

One tongue lashing from her mother, the mysterious reappearance of her diary, and a full suitcase later and Naz was on her way to dragon school. The Wyvold the Fierce School for Dragons had felt so foreign to her on the day of her entrance assessment that Naz was feeling pretty nervous.

Not that she was prepared to admit that to Sunni.

Naz sat at the base of her mother's neck, a beautiful violet dragon, her arms wrapped protectively around her little sister sitting in front of her. The journey home would be Sunni's first time on dragon back without Naz there to hold her. What if the younger girl fell off? She squeezed Sunni tighter to her chest at the thought.

The vibrantly coloured buildings, each with their roof embossed with the school crest, came into focus through Naz's flying goggles. The nerves that had been slowly bubbling in her stomach started boiling with full force and she thought she was going to retch.

Other dragons were winging their way towards the school too, the vivid hues of the fire dragons with their children upon their backs standing out in stark contrast to the more muted, yet stately, scales of the diminutive air dragons with their children in their arms. At the sight of her fellow pupils Naz swallowed the bile in her throat through sheer stubborn pride. She would *not* introduce herself to her new classmates with vomit splattered down her uniform.

With one final *whump whump* of her wings, Mrs Cinder landed on the grassy school oval with the other parents. Naz scrambled down her shoulder and had to dodge to the left when her suitcase came plummeting towards her from Sunni's outstretched arms.

'Gee, thanks,' she called, straightening up her uniform and pointedly refusing to take Sunni's hand to help her down.

'I was just trying to help. Lighten up.'

'Girls, girls,' Mrs Cinder said, now in her human form. 'Don't start.'

Sunni, ignoring her mother, was giving Naz a sweeping, assessing look. 'You look terrible,' she said.

'And here I was thinking how remarkably similar you two look to each other,' Mrs Cinder said sharply. 'Sunni, pipe down and don't be mean to your sister. It's her big day.'

She looked around her. 'None of the other parents seem to be going to the dorms - '

'It's fine, I know the way,' Naz said hurriedly. The last thing she needed was her mother holding her hand in front of her new dorm mates. 'I remember walking past it before my entrance assessment.'

'But I want to see inside the dorms.' Naz hated it when Sunni's voice took on that whine.

'You'll see them when it's your turn to go to Wyvolds,' their mother said, and Naz stuck her tongue out at Sunni.

'Stop that. Say goodbye to your sister properly.'

'Bye, jub jub brain,' Sunni said.

'Girls!' Mrs Cinder glared at the both of them. 'I want to see the two of you hug, or Sun Dragon preserve me I will - '

But they didn't get to hear the rest of the threat because, recognising that particular tone in their mother's voice, the sisters jumped in for a quick, awkward hug.

'That's more like it. To think how often dragons like to tell me how lucky I am to be blessed with two children when most are only fortunate enough to have one. Hah!' She held out her arms. 'Come, Nazish, hug your mother goodbye.'

Naz ran into her mother's open arms and gave her a proper farewell hug, suddenly not wanting to leave. 'I'll miss you,' she whispered so Sunni wouldn't hear.

'I'll miss you too, sweetheart.' She released Naz and straightened.

'Now, I had better not get any letters about you from the principal's office, you hear me?'

'Yes Mum.'

'Good. Now, off you go.'

Sunni was looking away and scrubbing suspiciously at her eyes when Naz turned back for a final goodbye. She gave her sister one last wave before lugging her suitcase across the grass, avoiding the dragons that were still landing, and followed the footsteps of the older pupils to the dormitories.

The other students, chattering excitedly away to each other, all made their way to a multi-coloured, tall building. Naz followed them in through the open doorway and noted the girls turned to their right, the boys to their left. She followed the girls and spotted a sign pointing to the Level 1 dorm rooms. Each door had a list of names pinned to it. She scanned them until she saw her own name and entered the room. The first to arrive, Naz had the choice of the four beds that sat in a row across one wall, each with its own desk, chest of drawers and cupboard. She selected the furthest bed from the door and dumped her suitcase on it. Another girl entered the room, an angry looking earth dragon with the palest skin Naz had ever seen. The other girl scowled in her direction, a look so reminiscent of Sunni that Naz felt like she wanted to cry. The earth dragon selected the bed closest to the door and furthest from Naz. This must be Diamond, judging from the list pinned to the dorm room door. Naz was spared having to make small talk by the arrival of two water dragons, Isla and Kairi, talking animatedly together. They each gave a shriek of joy when they saw that the two remaining beds were next to each other.

Naz busied herself with unpacking, feeling awful when no one made any move to talk to her. Her temper simmered to the surface at being ignored, and she went up to the two water dragons with her hand outstretched.

'I'm Naz,' she said, not bothering to keep her anger out of her voice.

'I'm Isla,' said the blonde girl, 'and this is Kairi.' The dark-haired girl next to her nodded hello.

'And your name is?' she said to the earth dragon. She and Diamond locked eyes, each as stubborn as the other.

Isla jumped into the breech. 'This is Diamond, or at least we think she is from the names on the door.'

Diamond shrugged her hefty shoulders and returned to her unpacking.

'You angry that you've been separated from your friends?' Naz asked Diamond.

'No.'

'I live so remotely, the only dragons I know are not in Level 1,' Naz said. 'So I guess you can say I'm excited to meet such a friendly dragon in my dorm.'

She would not let this earth dragon ignore her. 'Do you know anyone else in Level 1?'

The earth dragon rounded on her, but Naz refused to flinch despite their difference in size. 'What do you want?'

'I'm just wanna be friends, roomie,' she said, her hands held up in placation.

'Fine. We're friends. Now leave me alone.'

Naz gave her a wicked grin, the one she knew set Sunni's teeth on edge, and returned to her almost empty suitcase. After an awkward pause the water dragons resumed their babbling, and Diamond set about slamming her possessions into her drawers with great force. Naz smiled to herself. She would win Diamond over if it was the last thing she did. Earth dragons were notoriously angry, but they didn't scare her. Fire dragons were not without a temper themselves.

A bell sounded, and Naz dropped the last of her balled up socks into a drawer. 'Assembly time?' she asked the others. They shrugged but filed out of the room anyway. Naz pointedly walked next to Diamond but thought it would be a step too far to link her arm with the burly dragon.

Despite her determination, however, the dragon was able to shake her off in the throng of students once they made it to the assembly.

Refusing to be upset by it, she sat instead next to a square-faced water dragon with red-rimmed grey eyes.

'Hi, I'm Naz,' she said.

He gave her a watery smile. 'I'm Zhabiib, but everyone calls me Zeb.'

She grinned at him. 'Tell me who made you cry, and I'll bloody their nose for you.'

Zeb let out a surprised hoot of laughter. 'You'd punch the principal?'

'Of course, if it was for you,' Naz said. 'What'd he do?'

'He refused my best friend entry to the school. Says he has to mature a little more before he can come here.' Zeb gave a huge sniff.

Naz nodded understandingly. 'That sucks.'

'Do you know what I am going to do?' Zeb's square face set in determination. 'I'm going to deliberately fail every single one of my subjects so badly that they will have to keep me down a year. I will keep doing it, year after year, until they let my friend in.'

'It's as good a plan as any,' Naz said.

'You don't think I'm stupid?'

Naz shrugged. 'I don't know you well enough to know that yet, but if you *are* stupid, it would make your plan a whole lot easier.'

Zeb laughed again just as the crowd hushed and their principal, a tiny air dragon who looked remarkably like a turtle, walked out in front of them.

Naz winked at her new friend and settled down to listen to the boring man and his lecture on school rules.

CHAPTER TWO

FUN AND GAMES

'Okay the game is this,' Zeb whispered to Naz, leaning in so the other students around them wouldn't hear. 'We take in turns moving around the room. From wall to wall to wall. Whoever makes it the furthest before the teacher asks us to sit back down wins.'

Naz looked up at their teacher, a ditzy fire dragon called Mrs Byrne, who was sitting at her desk and correcting classwork. She rarely noticed whether or not the students were paying attention in class, so it would be a pretty easy game. She looked back at Zeb, who was smiling hopefully at her.

'You came up with the game, so I go first.'

'Of course.'

'And no calling attention to the teacher. We play fair or not at all.'

Zeb looked affronted. 'I'm not the one who plays unfair.'

Naz winked at him. 'I know.'

Slowly, carefully, Naz rose out of her seat and edged her way to the left-hand side of the room, where a bundle of cushions sat haphazardly along the wall. Diamond looked up at her curiously, but Naz just shrugged at her and the earth dragon returned to her work.

Naz, trailing her hand along the wall, made it all the way to the back wall before Kairi called out to the teacher.

'Mrs Byrne, Naz is out of her seat again.'

'Who?' Mrs Byrne looked up from the page, her brow furrowed in confusion. She looked around the room, her eyes finally alighting on Naz at the back of the room.

'Natasia, what are you doing back there?'

'Just trying to find a quiet space for some meditation, Mrs Byrne.'

'While that is a commendable activity, especially for one of your temper, Natasia, I really must insist that you go back to your desk. Examinations are not far away and you, of all dragons, need to study.'

Zeb's shoulders were shaking with laughter when Naz took her seat next to him.

'Did you put her up to it?'

'Who?'

'*Kairi.*'

'Nope. I just got lucky.' He rubbed his hands together. 'I sense victory, Cinder.'

Naz raised an eyebrow at him. 'For me, perhaps.'

Zeb waited until Mrs Byrne's focus was back on the papers in front of her before he took his turn. His chair squeaked as he pushed it back and Naz had to bite on her hand to stop her laughter. Mrs Byrne's head snapped up.

'Cyrus, where do you think *you're* going?'

Zeb held up his fist, his face the picture of innocence. 'To the bin, Mrs Byrne.'

'Well do so quietly. Some of us are trying to think calming thoughts.'

'Yes Mrs Byrne.'

He threw the scrunched-up piece of paper in the bin from where he stood and sat back down.

'Hah! I won,' Naz said.

'This time,' Zeb replied.

Naz sat on a cold, hard seat carved from stone, swinging her legs in a carefree manner. She snapped her fingers idly, watching the little sparks of pumpkin orange fire that shot out at every finger click. She gave a guilty start when a shadow loomed over her. Shaking away the last of the flames, Naz looked up at her burly Level 1 co-ordinator, Mr Ruffhead. He was leaning casually against the door of his office, but it was always impossible to tell how much trouble you were in with him. He was an expert at an impassive face. Only the slight twitching of his bulging muscles beneath his skin-tight shirt betrayed that he was annoyed to find her outside his office.

'Back again, Nazish?'

She hastened to pull a note out of her blazer pocket and handed it to him. He took it from her without comment and opened it up. He read its contents, a frown creasing his brow at the words. He folded the note back up with a sniff and still said nothing. He just stared at her, face impassive, until she started to squirm under his gaze.

'Do you have anything to say for yourself?' he asked.

'That depends on what the note says.' She cursed her big mouth the moment the words were out, but it was too late to take them back.

'A dragon of your intelligence should not be as close as you are to failing all of your classes,' he said. He started counting them off on his fingers. 'You have abysmal grades in Dragon Studies, despite coming to Wyvolds with a passable knowledge of the runes. Your grades are down in Fire Studies, and yet I can see that you have excellent control over your fire.' He looked meaningfully at the fingers she had been clicking when he had stepped out of his office. 'Need I go on?'

She couldn't bring herself to look at him. 'No, sir.'

The teacher sighed. 'What's going on, Naz? Is it boredom? We could have provided you with Level 2 work if you had let us know you were bored.'

When she didn't reply he came to sit on the stone chair next to her. It was a credit to the chair maker's craftmanship that the seat did not groan under his considerable bulk.

'You have formed a close friendship with Zhabiib Stream, I believe.'

'So?' Naz could feel the beginnings of her fire prickling beneath her skin.

'So Zeb is in serious danger of failing Level 1 as well. For a teacher, that is always a red flag that an unhealthy friendship has formed between some of our students.'

Naz folded her arms over her chest in an effort to hold in the fire that had flared brighter at his words.

'You cannot tell me who I can and cannot be friends with.'

'I can when I see so much potential going to waste.'

Naz's fire had reached her face and she knew her teacher would be able to feel it radiating from her skin, but to his credit he did not flinch away from her.

'If I keep receiving these complaints from your teachers, I will have no choice but to summon your mother to the school for a meeting so that some very serious decisions can be made about your future.'

He wouldn't dare! She looked up at him and saw he was being deadly serious, a rare hint of emotion etched across his face.

'I'll do better,' she said.

He nodded, but she could tell he did not believe her.

'You're to stay here for the rest of the lesson, and every other Personal Development lesson for the rest of the week,' he said, rising from his chair. 'Because I do not think it fair that Mrs Byrne should have to shoulder the burden of providing you with extra coursework, you will spend this Starsday in my office, catching up on your work instead of going to the village with your friends.'

'Yes, Mr Ruffhead,' was all she could manage to say with the fire still raging inside her.

The teacher returned to his office, leaving her to her own thoughts, and the fire within her gradually subsided to a gentle simmer, making it easier for her to think.

If her mother was summoned to the school Naz was a dead dragon walking, and Sunni would never let her live it down. But exams were only two weeks away. If she could keep her head down for a fortnight there would be no need for her mother to be involved at all.

Naz headed straight for her usual table at lunch, shoulders squared in determination. Zeb was already there, happily munching away at a plateful of fried shrimp.

'Naz!' he cried when he saw her. 'That was your best prank yet. It took us the entire lesson to get all the cushions off the roof. Your idea to use saddle glue was pure genius.'

Zeb's face fell when Naz didn't join in with his laughter. 'What's wrong?' he asked. He touched her arm and leapt backwards. 'Your skin is burning. What did Mr Ruffhead say to you?'

'Nothing. He was perfectly reasonable. I have to spend all Starsday doing schoolwork.'

'Oh. That's not so bad.' He eyed her cautiously.

'Not so bad? He's going to summon my mother if I get into any more trouble.'

She growled when Zeb's face showed no recognition at the threat behind her words.

'My mother is not a dragon to be trifled with, Zeb. I *cannot* have her up at the school.' She crossed her arms protectively across her chest. 'I can't get into any more trouble with you. Today was my last prank.' She forged ahead before she could lose her nerve. 'I don't think we should hang out together in class for a while.'

The prawn Zeb was eating fell out of his gaping mouth. 'You want to stop being my friend?'

'No, of course not,' she replied quickly. 'We're still friends, but I want to sit by myself in class from now on.'

Zeb nodded sadly and picked the fallen prawn up off the floor. 'I understand. Besides, next year we'll be in different year levels, anyway, so I won't be getting you into trouble anymore. Mr Ruffhead told me I'll definitely be kept back in Level 1.'

'You'll get to be with your best friend after all.' She couldn't bear Zeb's mortified expression at her waspish tone, so she swiped a beef sandwich from the platter on the table.

'I need to go walk off some of this fire before our next class starts. I'll catch you later.'

She headed out into the overcast afternoon, not giving him a chance to reply. She needed to make some sort of sense out of her whirling thoughts.

What was she going to do? Despite all her clowning around, Naz's school grades were not actually that bad. She was an intelligent dragon, and her mother had taught her a lot of the Wyvolds curriculum before the school year had even begun.

Naz bit into her sandwich, but it felt like ash in her mouth. Her mother would kill her if she failed. She headed for the school orchard, walking past Isla and Kairi. The water dragons were giggling over a notebook they were passing back and forth between them, their heads pressed together. The water dragons were, as always, completely unaware that Naz was there. They would be all she would have for company for the rest of her time at Wyvolds once Zeb got his wish to stay back in Level 1.

The years stretched ahead of her. They looked lonely and bleak.

Examination fever hit Wyvolds with full force and Zeb seemed to be the only student in the entire school who was not nervous. He reclined in his chair with his hands behind his head and his eyes closed during their Dragon Studies written examination, oblivious to the scowls thrown his way by the other students in Level 1. Naz answered the paper confidently, her pen strokes for the runes smooth and even. Her Magical Education practical examination did not go so well, and she struggled to perform the simple healing spell under Miss Hobstone's watchful gaze, but she knew she had made up for it in the written portion of the examination. Down in the Weaponry Dome, swinging swords against Diamond in their Hopology examination, Diamond's wooden sword hit Naz's with a *thwang* that reverberated throughout her entire body. She fell to her knees, oblivious to Diamond's follow-up swing, and was hit square in the forehead. She didn't have to see Mr Ruffhead's shake of his head to know she had not passed his subject, but she did not need Hopology to make it to Level 2.

All in all, Naz knew she had managed to claw her way back to a passable set of grades. Her mother would not be able to fault her and her efforts at all.

Naz's last examination was Transformation with the kindly air dragon, Mrs Stacey. Nerves started their sickly fluttering in her chest as she began the long walk across the soft grass to the tiny air dragon, who was already on the oval waiting for her.

'You know what to do, Naz. Just take your time,' Mrs Stacey said quietly.

Naz closed her eyes to hide her guilt. She stood there for a long time, indecisive, not yet trying to find the inner trigger that would begin her transformation. Failure to transform in this examination was an instant ticket to repeating Level 1, no matter how well she had done in her other classes.

'I-I'm sorry. I can't,' Naz said to her teacher before she could change her mind.

Mrs Stacey's brown eyes were filled with pity. 'That's okay, Naz,' she said. 'Many dragons take several years to be able to transform. It's perfectly normal. You can return to the school now.'

Naz nodded sadly and made her way back to her dorm. She lay down on her bed and refused to talk to anyone. What she had just done was irreversible. She shut her eyes. Visions of her mother's angry face invaded her thoughts, and Naz felt ill. Sunni's taunting face chased her mother's annoyed one and Naz groaned. She might be in the same year level as Sunni next year. She hadn't even considered that. What had she done?

She felt her bed dip and she opened her eyes to find Diamond sitting on the edge of the counterpane, her face stony.

'You did not manage to transform in your exam.'

Naz shook her head.

'I saw you transform on the oval last week when I came to find out where you had gone. You had deep red scales that shimmered in the dying sun light.' She kept her voice quiet and, to Naz's astonishment there was no anger in it. 'I'll miss you, but I understand why you did it.'

'What do you mean?' She examined Diamond's hard face properly for the first time. It held no malice, nor even contempt.

'Zeb,' Diamond replied. 'You two are close and there is no way he can pass Level 1, not with the way he has been acting.'

'Please don't tell anyone.'

Diamond gave a shrug of her huge shoulders. 'Who would I tell?'

Naz reached out her hand, but the earth dragon rose to her feet. 'Maybe now I'll get a decent roommate,' she said, but she grinned at Naz as she walked away.

'Maybe I will too,' Naz murmured.

If she had been nervous during her Transformations examination, Naz was positively anxious - nay terrified - now. The first of the parents had arrived to pick up their children for the summer holidays and Naz was waiting beside her suitcase for her mother to arrive. Zeb had wanted to wait with her for moral support, but Naz had not let him.

'She'd probably eat you. Not being family won't stop her,' she told him. With one last worried glance at the sky, he agreed. But then his face broke out in a grin.

'I guess I'll be seeing you next year,' he said. Despite her nerves she laughed.

'Yeah, I guess so.' She kept her eyes on the sky while they talked.

'I have to go to Mr Ruffhead's office as soon as I arrive next year. He's putting together an action plan so I don't fail again.'

'He's a clever dragon, Mr Ruffhead.'

Naz thought she spied a flash of purple among the throng of dragons winging their way to the school. 'You better go,' she said. She grabbed him into a quick hug and shooed him on his way.

With a look of grave concern on his face, Zeb gave her one last wave before going to the school lake to wait for his father.

Naz thought she was going to be sick at the familiar *whump whump* of her mother's wings as she landed on the grass. Sunni jumped down from their mother's back, her face serious. 'Mum doesn't want to transform here. We're to go straight home. Let me help you with your suitcase.'

Bile rose in Naz's throat. She had been hoping to have this confrontation in public. And why was Sunni being so nice? Her mother must have murder in mind for Sunni to have that look of pity on her face. She allowed her sister to help her hoist her suitcase onto their mother's back before climbing up the scaly leg herself and taking her place behind her. She didn't even dare ask Sunni if she was in trouble. Her mother had the hearing of a bat, and it would be even worse for her if she overheard Naz discussing her failure.

Mrs Cinder launched herself into the sky and winged her way home, the distance doing nothing to cool Naz's panic. The flight had felt long at the beginning of the year, but now it was far too short for Naz's liking. They were landing out the front of their home much too soon. Naz picked up her suitcase and followed Sunni inside while their mother transformed. She stood waiting in the kitchen for the tongue lashing she was certain was coming. Sunni made herself scarce, to Naz's relief.

Mrs Cinder entered the kitchen and examined her daughter for a long time, her arms crossed and her face neutral. Naz could not tell if this was a good sign or not.

'Would you like a cup of tea?' Mrs Cinder asked, and Naz gaped at her.

'You're not going to yell at me?'

Mrs Cinder huffed and grabbed the kettle off the stove. 'What would be the point in that?' She filled the kettle with water and lit the stove with a spark of fire from her fingertips.

'Naz, take a seat.'

Her entire body quivering, she did as her mother asked. Her mother took a seat opposite her.

'Naz, it's okay that you didn't manage to transform. It's common and you will find many of your peers didn't manage it either.'

'Oh.' Naz didn't know what else to say.

'Naz, you're an incredibly intelligent young woman,' her mother said. 'The updates I have been receiving from school are not like you at all.' She paused. 'Except for the wilful defiance bit, but then you are my daughter.' She scrubbed a hand over her face.

'I hope I have not taught you to fear failure,' she said. 'Trying and failing is how we learn, it's how we improve. You cannot expect to get everything right first time around.'

'I'll try harder next year, I promise.'

The kettle started whistling on the stove and her mother got up to make the tea. 'I know you will.' She set a cup down in front of Naz.

'This water dragon friend of yours. He *is* just a friend, isn't he?'

'Mum!' Naz stared at her mother owlishly.

Her mother held her hands up as if in protest of her innocence. 'Just checking,' she said. 'Besides, after the year you have had you are to have no boyfriends until you have finished your studies. The last thing you need is the distraction.'

'Well, that's an easy promise to make. They're a dull lot, the boys in my year.'

Her mother grinned knowingly. 'There's no denying you're my daughter alright. Now finish your tea and then go and unpack.'

'Yes Mum.'

'Oh, and Naz?' The nerves returned at the tone of her mother's voice. 'You are grounded for the entire summer holiday. Gluing cushions to the ceiling of your Personal Development classroom? You're lucky I didn't fly down to the school and wallop you in front of your entire school for that one.'

Naz gulped down the last of her tea and hurried from her mother's sight before she could change her mind about not walloping her. Facing an entire summer with no company except for Sunni, Naz hoped with all her might that her new classmates next year would be worth it.

'Just one fire dragon I can get along with, that's all I ask,' she muttered to herself as she pulled her belongings out of her suitcase.

'Pfft, as if,' Sunni said from her bed, looking up from the book she was reading. 'I don't think you have it in you to get along with anyone.'

'Shut up, Sunni.'

'I've missed you too, Naz,' her sister replied with sickly sweetness, before turning her attention back to her book.

Naz smiled to herself as she finished her unpacking. It was good to be back at home, her troubles passed for now, and a fresh new year on the horizon.

ACKNOWLEDGMENTS

Rachaya and her friends would never have come into existence if not for Steve and his never ending support. Thank you for everything.

To my very first beta readers, Kate Sekiya, Jessica Vander Reyden and Rhys Oldfield, your encouragement and enthusiasm meant the world to me and your insights have helped shape the entire series.

To Ben Rawlings, Jen Bourne, Chelsea Bourne, Luciana Carvalho, Liz O'Brien and the students at St Joeseph's Primary School; your feedback was hugely helpful and very much appreciated.

To my wonderful editor, Kat Betts of Element Editing Services, you have done such a fantastic job. Thank you for your professionalism and expertise. I hope to work with you again on future projects.

To Vin and Rosemary for your constant support, your shelter, and the regular gossip sessions over wine. You're very much appreciated.

Lastly, thank you to Mum and Dad for all the books. You must have spent a small fortune over the years pandering to my passion. Thank you for fostering my imagination and for the unconditional love.

OTHER BOOKS BY ASH OLDFIELD

Ash Oldfield is a fantasy fiction and children's writer from Melbourne, Australia. She is the author of *The Rachaya Series* and has several short works of fiction in various publications.

When she is not working on her latest piece of fiction, Ash enjoys drinking good coffee, taking her dog for walks on the beach and hanging out with her two cats.

Sign up for monthly emails and get a free Rachaya series short story, visit: bit.ly/3tdevUs

Giving the book a review on Amazon is a great way to support my writing. You can leave me a review here:

www.azonlinks.com/B07651KPDG

www.AshOldfield.com